TROUBLE ON THE HILL

nd other stories

y Michael Glenn

Trouble on the Hill

a collection
of short stories

by Michael Glenn

Liberator Press   Chicago, Illinois

ISBN   0-930720-61-X
Library of Congress Catalog Card Number: 79-88413

Manufactured in the United States of America
Liberator Press
Chicago, ILlinois

Contents

Dakota Story

I'm still not sure why they asked me to go along. Maybe because I had a car. Or maybe because they somehow wanted at least one white person to go with them, anticipating what they'd be up against from the judge. Or maybe cause Pete felt closer to me than I'd thought at the time. I don't know. In any case, I agreed to go; and at seven that morning, even though it was snowing up a storm, I picked them both up at their apartment, and we headed out across the Dakota flatlands hugging to the road in the swirling snow and hoping to hell the Dodge would make it.

"Do you think the court will be open?" Aleena asked.

"I don't know," I said. "Usually the judge won't go out if the weather's bad."

"We have to go," Pete said. "If we don't show up, they'll throw the case out of court, and that will be that."

"And what if we show up and the judge doesn't?" Aleena said.

"Then they'll reschedule it."

"You can never tell," I said. "If the judge lives nearby, he might come."

"We don't have a choice," Pete said.

We settled in for the drive, all of us in the front seat to keep warm. I turned the heat on full blast, got some music on the radio to try and help us relax, and hunched forward so I could see the road better.

It was a bitter day. The plastic frost shields on the windows were iced up, and the windshield wiper blades kept skipping over chunks of frozen snow, making a grating sound, until it would get so bad, we'd have to stop to fix them. The guy on the radio said it was five degrees, but with the wind-chill factor, it must have been fifteen below. And the wind was getting stronger as the day moved on.

I had met Pete at a rap center in town. It was the only place young people had to hang out, and you could always find a couple high school kids, folks from the community college like myself, and a few lonely Air Force men there. Pete had come in out of curiosity at first and had been surprised at the warm atmosphere inside. He was a good guitar player, and a lot of us would gather around him and listen to him improvise around the latest popular songs. For a while he was coming regularly. The night we had our all night "heart-to-heart" meeting, he was there, and that was when I got a sense of how strongly he felt about what had happened to his people, and how hard it was for him to trust any of us.

We urged him to accept us as his friends. Soon afterwards, he invited us to a traditional pow-wow on the Reservation. We were guests of honor there, and although the people were dirt poor, they gave us the best they had. It was a solemn occasion, the old men chanting and beating the drums and wailing in their highpitched tones. At the end of the evening they asked us to dance for them.

"I know you don't know how," Pete had whispered. "But it would be a great insult if you refused."

And so we'd all gotten up and tried to dance what we were

feeling, some of us imitating the Indian dances we'd seen, others dancing the kind of steps they were most at home with. However awkward we were, it seemed to go over all right with our hosts, because they stood up and applauded as we moved past them. From then on, though, Pete came by the center less and less. I knew he was working pretty hard at the music store in town, but that couldn't have been the whole story. When I'd meet him on the street, he'd be friendly, but reserved.

I didn't know Aleena much at all. She'd never come by the center like Pete had; and, from what I knew, she kept pretty much to herself and her people. She and Pete had been married just over a year. That's why I was surprised when he called me up and asked if I'd go with them. He said we had to go help Aleena's sister.

After we'd got about ten miles outside of town, I turned to them both and said, "Tell me what's going on. I don't even know what this is all about."

"Okay," Pete said. "They're trying to take Mary's boy away. They say she isn't a good mother. They're having the court hearing today to decide on it."

"What makes them say she's not a good mother?"

"I don't understand it all," Pete said. "Something the doctor wrote."

"It doesn't matter," Aleena said. "They don't need any reason. They take children away from us all the time. Send them to boarding schools. Send them to white families. And we never see them again."

"That's true," Pete said quietly. "I've known a lot of people it's happened to."

It was about a two hour drive, and nobody had much to say. I was trying to concentrate on the road. We stopped one place for coffee and doughnuts and so I could wipe the windshield off from top to bottom. The woman at the counter said we were crazy to be on the road 'cause a blizzard was blowing up, and I told her we'd skidded a few times already but nothing too serious. It turned out she knew my aunt up in Velva and asked me to say hello next time I saw her. Then she was telling us, "Thank you much," and we were back on the road.

By this time the snow was about three or four inches deep on the road and blowing every which way. When it gusted up, I had to slow down because I couldn't see. Everything was white: the sky, the road, the fields. You got a headache if you stared at it too long. I had to keep looking at the dashboard or down at Pete's dark pants to get my eyes back in shape.

"Pete. A lot of the kids at the center really miss you," I said. "Especially that guitar." I hesitated.

"Well. I got work to do," he said.

"But after work. . . ."

"After work he spends time with his family," Aleena said. "I don't want him going out at night. He works hard all day, sometimes ten or eleven hours. And I'm working, too. We want some time together."

"Where are you working?"

"I clean the rooms in the hotel."

"Well, I just. . . ."

"It's not just that," Pete said. "The kids at the center, they're just too young. None of them are married. They like to kid around, flirt. That's not for me any more. You know?"

"Yeah. I can understand what you're saying."

I turned my attention back to the road. When a cross wind cut across the highway, the visibility was reduced to a few feet, and I had to slow down until we were out of it.

By 9:30, half an hour before the case was supposed to start, we reached the county courthouse in Stanton. Aleena's sister would be waiting there for us.

Stanton is a little town on the Knife River, about two miles from the Missouri. I'd never been there before, but it reminded me of dozens of other towns in the Dakotas, the kind you drive through in a minute, prairie on one side and prairie on the other. The streets were almost empty because of the blizzard, the only moving things being front loaders and police cars. I dropped Pete and Aleena off at the courthouse, and then put the Dodge into a parking place with an electric plug so the engine wouldn't crack, and started walking back to find them.

The courthouse was a fairly new building. I went inside and looked around. Pete and Aleena were standing with another woman outside the door to the clerk's office. They looked so helpless, the three of them standing together in the corridor, against the stone pillars and legal yellow walls, so clearly out of place in the white man's house, that for a minute I saw them not as my two friends and their sister, but as three Indians. They would have been any three Indians for all I knew. Mary, who I'd never met, was short and stout, with dark coppery skin and long black hair. She was wearing a tattered overcoat, cracked shoes and men's woolen socks. Her face was all knotted up. I could see she'd been crying. Aleena suddenly looked a lot like her sister. For all her better clothes and slimmer figure, she presented the same heavy features: broad nose, firm full mouth, and large deepset penetrating brown eyes. The two women were standing the same way, too, as if to emphasize their relationship.

Pete was between the two of them, like he was protecting them, but I could see he felt uneasy, not knowing what to do or what to expect. I remembered him telling me horror stories of the way his people had been treated by the police and the courts, and the B.I.A., and, all of a sudden feeling that I wanted to be with them, I walked over to them, trying to look confident so they'd feel better.

"Well?"

"Howie. This is Mary," Pete said.

We shook hands. "Glad to know you," I said. "What's the story?"

Pete reached in his pocket and brought out a letter written to Mary by the court. "This is what they sent her."

I looked at it. It was a notice of the proceedings to determine foster home placement for Mary's boy. It was signed by the clerk of the court, whose door we were standing outside.

"Let's go in," I suggested.

We knocked on the door, then opened it and went in. As soon as they saw us, the clerks and secretaries gave us the once over. You know how people can put someone "in their place" with a look? Well, this is what these people did. They didn't say a word, but it was all clear in a few seconds.

"Can I help you?" one of the women asked in a pleasant voice that wasn't pleasant.

6

We asked her about the court case.

"I'm sorry. But Judge Beltim has cancelled all his cases for the day on account of the weather."

We looked at one another.

"What does that mean?"

"There is no court today. You'll be notified when the next date is set."

"Figures," Pete muttered.

"How's that?" the woman asked.

"Nothing."

"You'd better get back on the road," one of the officers said. "It's blowing up pretty bad. They say it's going to get worse."

"Right," I said. "Okay. Thanks."

We walked back outside the clerk's office.

"Now what?" I said.

Aleena's sister said something in Lakotah. I realized she didn't speak much English. Then she started crying.

"What'd she say?" I asked.

"She wants her boy."

"Where is he now?"

She asked, then translated Mary's answer. "In the hospital. The doctor has him under observation until the case is settled."

"How long has he been there?" I asked, sensing before I got my answer that it was a long time.

"Three months."

"Jesus! How old is he?"

"Just over two years."

I didn't know what to say.

"That's why Mary's crying. She says she misses him a lot. She wants him home. The apartment is empty without him."

I looked at Pete. He was red in the face and rigid, clenching and unclenching his fists.

"Is this the same doctor who wrote the letter?"

"Uh-huh."

"Well," I blurted out. "Why don't we do something. Where's this doctor at? Why don't we at least go talk to him?"

They looked at one another and talked Lakotah for a minute or so.

"The hospital is in Elbowoods. That's on the Reservation. If you want to take us there, she'd like to go."

"It's fine with me. Otherwise the day's a total waste."

"It's not that far."

We pulled our coats around us and headed outside again, ducking our heads when we hit the wind. It was a blizzard, all right. The snow blew into every crack in your clothing, down your neck, into your socks, underneath your gloves. It was really cold. The first blast of air let you know that your whole face would be numb if you stayed out a couple minutes.

We ran to my car, and I opened the door so everyone could get in, then unplugged the engine heater and climbed in myself. I got the motor going and cleared the inch or so of fresh snow off the windshield. "Let me get some gas," I said, "and then we'll be off."

"Okay."

"How did your sister get here this morning?"

"One of her friends who works in town."

"Oh." I pulled into the town's one gas station, got the tank filled up, and then we were on the highway again.

We crossed the Missouri, then headed north towards Garrison Lake, the largest man-made lake in the world, after which we'd turn west towards the reservation.

The heat in the car started making us drowsy. Pete, who hadn't said much on the trip down, began talking in a low voice, reflectively. "All of this used to be our land," he said, sitting next to me. "Mandan. Hidatsa. Arikara. Our people farmed this valley for centuries. Now the lake has flooded the best land, and the white man has pushed us into a tiny area of what we had, and where the land is poor."

"What can you do about it?" I asked.

"I don't know," he said. "Some want to fight. Others want to file all these legal suits to try and get our land back. But I don't think the legal suits will win. After all, look who controls the courts."

"How do you *feel* about it?"

He sighed. "I want a life for Aleena and me. A family. A steady job. I'd like to get some more education, like you and some of the others at the center, but I don't think that's possible now. Where would I get the money?"

"Maybe later," I said.

"I doubt it." He paused. "But sometimes," he went on, "I feel like I can't go on with things the way they are. You see what it's like on the reservation. All the men, drinking their lives away. The families torn apart. The children going without education. The diseases. No one wants to stay on the reservation any more. People want to go to Minneapolis, Chicago, even further. But as soon as they get away, we hear that things are no better for them. They can't find jobs. The discrimination is just as bad in the city. Some of them even come back, defeated in their hopes." He took a deep breath. "So I don't know."

"It takes a lot of courage to keep on going," I said.

"I'm tired of courage alone, without any changes in the world out there," he said brusquely, waving his hand at the blinding white prairie. "Every minute of our lives is run by someone else."

"Uh-huh."

He was quiet for a minute. I stared at his face, noticing how pitted his skin was; then, sensing the car slide beneath me, I quickly concentrated on the road.

"I just want to get that boy back for Mary. That's all I want to do," he said.

"Then let's do it."

Just past Coleharbor, we made our cut to the west, paralleling the Missouri, and headed for the Fort Berthold Reservation. I picked up a Minot radio station, and we listened to it until we reached Elbowoods.

By the time we arrived, it was close to eleven. It felt colder. Mary pointed out the doctor's office, and we climbed out of the car and headed up the path, then rang the bell.

The doctor opened the door himself. He was a young man, in his early thirties. From his accent, I figured he was from the northeast. He was wearing a short white jacket, dark trousers, shirt and tie.

"Mary," he said. "Come in. What can I do for you? Have you been to the court?"

"I'm Mary's sister, Aleena," Aleena said, pushing forward. "This is my husband, Pete."

"And I'm a friend, Howie," I said, reaching out to shake hands.

"Come in. Come on, all of you," he said. "My goodness. It's a dreadful storm out there, isn't it?"

He helped us off with our coats and ushered us into his office. There was a smell of rubbing alcohol and soap. On one side of the room was an examining table, covered by a white sheet, with a scale and a floor lamp beside it. The other side of the room was taken up by the doctor's desk, a small bookcase piled high with paperbound medical books and magazines, and several wooden folding chairs.

He opened up four of the folding chairs for us and placed them in a small semicircle around the desk. Then he crossed to his own chair, sat down, and, leaning back, lit up his pipe. We all sat down. "Now, what is it?" he said.

"We've been to the court," Aleena said. "But the hearing was cancelled. So we decided to come and talk to you about Mary's baby."

"All right."

He was an earnest-looking man with a sharp chin and clear blue eyes. His face was very smooth. His fingers seemed almost too delicate. A sudden gust of wind sent a shower of frozen pellets hammering against the windows.

"What can I tell you?" he asked.

Mary suddenly burst into tears, rocking back and forth, and moaning. She was like a dam that had burst. She couldn't stop.

The doctor's face got red. He didn't know what to do. "Mary, Mary," he kept repeating, leaning forward, trying to pat her hand. "Mary, what is it?"

She pulled her hand away from him and wrapped it tightly with her other one. For a long time it seemed nothing could get her to stop. Pete and Aleena stared straight ahead.

Finally she quieted down long enough to blurt out, "I want my baby back."

The doctor smiled. "Why, of course," he said soothingly. "And you *will* have him back. Why are you crying so?"

"She's crying because you want the court to take him away," Aleena said. "You want him sent to a foster home. That's not giving him back to his mother."

"Yes, I do want him sent to a foster home," the doctor said. But only for a short period of time." He gestured with his palms up. "And then he'll be coming back to live with his mother. And he'll be stronger when he comes back. And healthier."

Mary said something in Lakotah.

"She says, if he goes to a foster home, he'll never come back," Aleena said.

"Nonsense. He'll go for a period of three months, to get healthier. And then he'll be coming back home."

Aleena translated it for her sister, who answered angrily.

"She says, she's seen lots of babies taken away to foster homes. And almost none of them came back. She says they wind up in boarding homes, or white people's homes. But they don't come back to the reservation."

The doctor shook his head. "I can't believe that," he said. "I know some children, for their own good, may be separated from their families. But I think that happens to just a few. And, certainly, that wouldn't be my intent with little Tony. . . ."

"Just what *is* your intent, doctor?" I said. "Why does the boy have to go at all?"

He seemed almost relieved to be able to explain. "It's a simple medical problem. We call it 'failure to thrive.' What this means is, Tony has just not been gaining the height or the weight he should be gaining. He's small for his age. And he is slow, mentally." He lit his pipe again, sending a sweet, pungent aroma into the air. "We examined him and observed him in the hospital. Mary, isn't that the truth? He's quite small for his age. And he can't do many things other boys his age can do."

Aleena translated it for her. She nodded. "That's true," she said. "But it's no problem. I can take care of him." She began crying again. "I want him home with me."

"Why do you think he'd be better in a foster home?" I asked.

"It's hard to say. For one thing, his mother is poor, and she can't afford to feed him a well-balanced diet."

"That's not her fault," Aleena said sharply.

The doctor gestured at her. "I know that. I know. But let me finish. His diet is one of the reasons he's small. The foster home would feed him better and build him up physically. And there are other factors. Other children to learn from. A foster mother who is experienced in dealing with young children, whereas this is Mary's first child. A stable home atmosphere. This isn't to blame Mary for the problem. It's just that Tony would do better in a foster home."

"None of what you say makes any sense," Aleena answered.

"Just a minute," he said, waving his hand again. He didn't seem used to being disagreed with. "I only recommended a three month placement. She'd have him back after that. And, believe me, he'd be a lot stronger. A lot stronger." It was like he was pleading his case.

"It would be unusual if she got him back," Pete said, breaking his silence. "Maybe you don't understand how things work around here. If she got him back, I'd be very surprised."

"So would I," Aleena said.

"Well, then, perhaps I'm the one who doesn't understand," the doctor said. "Perhaps you should explain it to me."

"It's simple," Pete said. "You take the baby out of the home. Put him in a hospital for three months. Then you put him in a foster home for three months. All this time, his mother is upset. When the time comes for him finally to go home, the social worker writes a little note. 'I wonder if this mother is stable enough to accept the responsibilities of her child,' she says. She talks about how unhappy Mary has been. She says she asked Mary to see a psychiatrist, but Mary said no. Mary was 'hostile.' Now she is 'withdrawn' as well. The social worker ends up by saying she thinks Mary is 'mentally ill.' She recommends another three to six months in the foster home for the child, who she says is doing fine. Not like he was doing in the dirty Indian home, you understand. This is a clean home."

The doctor was listening.

"So the court decides to leave the boy there for three more months. It asks Mary to seek therapy, but she refuses. And so on it goes. Mary gets worse and worse. The boy does well where he is. And they never see each other again." He turned away. Then he leaned towards the doctor and banged his fist down hard on the desk. *"Now* do you understand?"

"I hear what you're saying. But," he stammered, "I can't believe this is what they do here."

"This is the *reservation*, doctor," Aleena said.

"It's true, I've only been here for six months," he said. "But. . . ."

The room was quiet. Outside, the snow whirled madly against the windows, cascading down in spiral sheets against the house, the road, the trees, the fields, trying to cover everything in its sterile whiteness. The wind rattled the windowpanes. A sudden draft made me shiver.

"I can't believe this is what they do," he went on. "I've sent children to foster homes before. The courts have seemed genuinely concerned to me. There hasn't been any trouble."

"Have the children come back home?"

The doctor paused. "Well, to be honest. . . ." He paused. "I don't really know. I haven't been here long enough to follow up." He paused again, a flush spreading over his face.

"I'd suggest you try to find out," Aleena said. "Maybe you'd be surprised."

The doctor rubbed his upper lip with his right hand. He frowned. "I mean, I've been very busy practicing medicine here. There's so much to do. . . .I haven't had that much contact with the courts, the social workers."

"The B.I.A.," Pete said. "That's who makes the rules."

The doctor hesitated. "Mary," he said, his voice shaky. "Is this really so? Is this what you think will happen?"

Aleena translated.

"Yes," Mary said.

The doctor sighed. "And you think I would do all this, deliberately, to you?"

Aleena translated it again.

"Yes."

It was like a knife in his side. The doctor twisted in his seat, a pained, shocked look on his face. "You think I'd deliberately tear your family apart? After I've come here, just to help your people, to do what I can do. . . ." His mouth hung open, jaws slack. "I'm just trying to do the best I can," he said in a small voice.

Aleena didn't bother translating. "This is our experience," she said. "Perhaps you didn't understand. But this is how things happen here."

The doctor stared in front of him, his features suddenly paler than pale. His pipe lay on the desk. His lips twitched, but he didn't say anything. He was quiet for a long time.

Outside, a powerful gust of wind sent snowflakes rattling against the windowpanes again. The whole house shook, and for an instant, it was like something whistling, howling and beating with its fists on the siding.

"This is just too confusing," the doctor finally said, almost in a whisper. "If this is what all of you think. . . ." He shook his head without saying anything, his face all knotted up. It was clear he was going through some inner turmoil.

"I don't know," he blurted out. "If all this is true, then maybe I should just leave the reservation. I came here to provide some decent medical treatment, but now. . . ." He paused.

I glanced at Pete. He was looking at his hands, squeezing his thick fingers, playing with the nails.

"I don't know *what* to do," the doctor said. "I just don't want to be in the middle of all this!"

His whole reason for coming to the reservation had gone sour.

"Maybe I should just leave," he said again.

"What about the boy?" Aleena said.

The doctor waved his hand. "I'll take care of that. I'll write another letter to the court, saying he's well enough to go back to his mother." He shook his head again. "I'm not what you think I am. I came here to do something good, not something bad. I'm not an animal. . . ."

"No one thinks you're an animal," Aleena said quietly. She turned and translated what he had said for her sister.

Mary began crying again. "Thank you," she said. "Thank you."

"Don't thank me," the doctor said. "Maybe I should thank you. I'm just sorry I caused you so much unhappiness. Really, I had no idea. I haven't had that much contact. . . ."

Mary said something in Lakotah.

"She says she thinks you're a good doctor," Aleena said. "She thinks it would be wrong for you to leave."

"One doctor's not the problem," Pete muttered.

"But it's clear from talking to you," the doctor said. "The situation's more complicated than I realized. I feel like I thought I was doing one thing, but maybe in fact I was doing another."

"You think you'd be better off back East?" I said.

The wind answered with a mighty blast, pushing and pulling the windows in their frames.

"Maybe," the doctor said. "At least I'd know where I was and what I had to deal with."

"And who do you think would take your place?" Aleena said angrily. "Maybe no one. Then we wouldn't have any doctor until the next term began. Maybe someone who understands as little about us as you did when you came here. It's foolish to leave just because you were wrong."

"Mmm. I see what you mean," the doctor said. He sighed. "I've just got to think it over."

"If we had our own doctors, it wouldn't be a problem," Pete said.

"Well. I *will* think it over. I will," the doctor said. "And I'll send the letter off to the court immediately. With a copy to the social worker. So that Mary can get her baby back."

The room was quiet once again.

"Well. Maybe we'd better get back," I said. "Or else we might not make it."

I stood up. So did the others. The doctor walked us to the door, holding Mary by the arm. We put our coats on again, and he opened the door for us.

"Good-bye. I'm glad that you came. Really I am."

"Good-bye. Thanks, doc."

"Thank you."

"So long."

"Good-bye."

We walked out quickly, pulling our coats around us as the wind bitterly assailed us, spraying snow down our necks and backs, and blasting our faces with freezing air.

And then we were in the car again, bucking the snow, the heaters turned all the way up. We dropped Mary off and started the long drive home. Aleena tried to sleep in the back seat. Pete and I sat in the front.

For a while nobody said anything.

"Do you think he'll stay?" I finally asked.

"I don't care what he does," Pete said. And he didn't say anything else for about fifty miles.

Barney

"Barney?" Will said. "He was a good ol' guy. One of the best. Oh, I don't know if he was any dif'rent from you or me. He had his days. Sometimes he'd be full of jokes and playin' tricks. Other days he'd be angrier'n hell. I guess he wasn't no better or no worse'n anybody else.

"I 'member when he started workin' here. Twenty-three years ago. He'd just got laid off a job in some garage. So he came over to the plant an' started up on the line in the body shop. 'I'm only going to be here a couple months,' he says. 'When my ol' job opens up, I'm goin' right back.' Then his ol' job opened up, but by then he was pals with the other guys and makin' more money here'n he would've there. 'What the hell,' he says, 'I'll make a go of it on the line, save up some money and start up my own damn garage.' So he stayed on an' that was that.

"Well, he never left. We'd kid him about it, but then a lot of other guys had an idea of savin' up some money and makin' it on their own, too. Buyin' a farm. Buyin' a store. Somewhere. A couple of them—Danny, Clyde Harris—tried it. I don't think it worked out too good. Danny came back. Clyde Harris wound up in some other factory, Pete. . .what was his last name. . . Ruperson, I think. He made it into some kind of rug business. But not that many guys leave. It's sort of a hope that keeps you goin' day after day, feelin' you're not really chained to the line when deep down you know you are. But no, Barney never left.

"I 'member we was workin' together for a while down in the paint shop. Oh, Jesus, we was a tough crew of sons-o'-bitches. Hawes was foreman there. Barney 'n me 'n the others, we'd give him fits.

"One day, Barney goes up to the roof, right durin' work, and everyone else comes along. We start doin' exercises up there, all of us, like it was a gym or somethin'. When Hawes finally finds us, one guy's runnin' aroun' the roof doin' laps. Two guys are havin' a wrestlin' match. Barney is standin' on his head in the corner. Oh, Jesus! Hawes takes one look at everyone and then shakes his head. 'I don't believe it,' he says. 'Tell me I don't see what I'm seein'.' Barney, he just keeps on standin' on his head, never says a word. Hawes was bullshit.

"But we'd do things like that. Later, Barney fixed himself a place where he could sleep and no one could find him. It was a regular game him and Hawes played. Well, Barney had this place, way up on top of a stack of boxes, in the back of the shop beyond the fender line near the railroad track. Anyway, he'd climb up there an' sack out for an hour or two. No one could find him.

"An' Hawes would be goin' 'round, 'You see Barney? Anyone see Barney?' 'Oh, yeah, I think he just went off to the john,' we'd say. 'Gone to take a leak.' 'Goddamit, I just *been* to the john,' Hawes'd say. 'Well, maybe he stopped by the supply shop,' we'd say. An' all the time he'd be in his room. He got it fixed up pretty good after a while. Even put in some curtains and got a radio. I asked him when he was goin' to get a water bed, but he'd just laugh. But he'd do things like that. Anythin' he could do to drive 'em crazy."

"I heard he had some problems at home," Davies said.

"Yeah. Like anyone else, I guess," Will answered. "You know how it is. Here he was, workin' second shift. His wife was workin' first shift. The kids don't never see him. His wife gets tired and bitched off. He goes off with the guys every night after work for a couple beers, an' when he gets home there's a fight. After he'd been workin' here about six years, they finally had it out. She packed up an' went off to her folks, an' he got royally drunk for a week an' finally went to see her, an' they both yelled at each other, an' then they cried an' promised to do better. So they both went back to it. What c'n you do? It's the workin' two shifts, you know what it's like. Messes up your family life. I don't know anyone it hasn't done somethin' to. You just got to learn to live with it, make the best of it. . . .

"He had a good bunch of kids. I'll say that. I was over his house a couple times. Two boys, bright as hell and tough as nails. An' a little girl, would take your heart away. They turned out okay. I think all of 'em are married now, livin' somewhere around here."

"I heard he was one of the leaders in the strike," Davies said.

"That's true. He was. One mornin' we was all out there packed up in our winter coats, knockin' our hands together to keep warm, drinkin' coffee like there was no tomorrow. We must've been out, I'd say, nine weeks, already. An' the company was talkin' scabs. And everybody was hungry and hurtin'. Anyway, a bunch of the guys said as how they figured we should go back, take the company offer and just get back to work. Christmas was comin' and people were feelin' pretty bad.

"Ol' Barney, he stood up. 'God dammit,' he says. 'I ain't been out for nine weeks now to go back with my tail 'tween my legs. If you say we're hurtin', think how the *company* must be hurtin'. So I say we stay out here 'til we get what we want an' c'n stick it right up their ass! An' if anyone wants to go back, I say we ought to break their legs before we see 'em cross the picket line.'

"He'd put everyone in their place talkin' like that. I mean, people respected him. He got himself on the strike committee even though he wasn't an officer in the union or anythin'. An', Jesus, he'd give 'em hell if they didn't run the strike like he thought it ought to be run. I think he saw through most of 'em pretty quick. Guys like 'The Rock' who talk out o' both sides o' their mouth at the same time, but were just in it for themselves. Barney, he spoke up for what the workers wanted. I don't think some of 'em liked him any more'n the company did, to tell the truth. 'Cause he'd push 'em right to the wall to keep 'em honest.

"But he wasn't ever in it for himself, if you know what I mean. After the strike, he could've run for the executive board or somethin', but he wouldn't. 'Hell,' he said, 'I got enough to do already.' He was like that. If there was a struggle goin' on, you could count on him to be there, all the way. But if things was goin' on as usual, he'd be like everybody else.

"He was in jail a couple times durin' the strike. But he didn't make anything out of it."

"Not like 'The Rock,' hmmm," Davies said. " 'The Rock' still talks about how he got beat up for the workers."

"Beat up, hell!" Will said. "He got pushed around by some cops an' shoved in the ribs. That was all. But every time union elections come up, you c'n be sure 'The Rock's' goin' to bring it up. Ol' timers like me 'member that 'The Rock' was all ready to sell us out, an' on more 'n one occasion. That's why we won't vote for him. Barney laid it out pretty good. 'He ain't no Rock.' An' the feelin' was mutual."

"What happened the day he died? I heard a lot of different stories," Davies said.

Will took a deep breath, then let it all out like a sigh. He pursed his lips and nodded and reached in his pocket for a cigarette. "Yeah," he said, "I was there. I c'n tell you what happened."

The younger man waited while he took a drag of the cigarette and blew the smoke out slowly, in a gray cloud which spiraled in lazy wisps to the ceiling.

"He shouldn't've been there in the first place. But the company refused to let him bid off the job. They were screwin' him over. I don't think they ever forgot what he did durin' the strike. Or how he'd always write 'em up when they wouldn't go by the book.

"But he was there, workin' in the lead booth. It's a bad job for a younger man, even. And not for somebody Barney's age. You got to wear an outfit that covers your whole body, special suit an' a mask an' hood. An' you still breathe in all them fumes. You sweat so much, your visor stays steamed up.

"He was there maybe eighteen months. He tried to bid off, but they said it was frozen. So you'd see him every day, wheezin' an' coughin', an' you'd know it was gettin' to him. But there wasn't nothin' you could do about it. An' nothin' he could do about it. That was going to be the way it was."

He took another drag off his cigarette and then squeezed the ash onto the floor with his thumb and forefinger. "There ain't much to say about it. The day he died, he was complainin' about pain in his chest. They sent him to the nurse, 'n she gave him one of those pain pills an' sent him back to the line. They didn't have enough pool men that day, an' they had to keep the line movin'. He asked 'em once again, could he go home. But Ryerson argued with him to stay on. At least 'til lunch. I don't know why, but he agreed. Maybe it was 'cause he always hated to take off for bein' sick. But he told me he was definitely goin' home after lunch if he didn't feel better.

"So he kept on workin', all steamed up, coughin', chasin' cars down the line. You could tell he was workin' slower 'n usual.

"An' all of a sudden, he was staggerin' out o' the lead booth. His hand was tight against his chest. He threw his hood off an' shouted he needed air. An' then he fell down. About three steps from the water fountain over there.

"Everyone stopped work an' ran over. But he was unconscious. He wasn't breathin'. An' there was some kind of blood or pink liquid, all bubbles like, comin' out o' his mouth 'n nose. Jesus, he looked awful. His face was all gray.

"I guess it took about five minutes for the company to get someone down there. They threw him on one of those stretchers an' rushed him off to the nurse's office in one of those electric trucks. He was dead when he got there, I think. But they sent him to the hospital anyway. I think it was so they could say he didn't die in the plant, but in the ambulance. That way, they get off payin' more insurance to his wife.

"But that was how it happened. A few minutes later, they had someone else in the lead booth doin' his job.

"The guys was pretty angry. But then the company said as how he was fifty years old, an' people his age had heart attacks whether they worked on the line or not, an' there wasn't any connection between the work he did and how he died. They even got the company doctor to go around, backin' 'em up. You know how they are when they want to do something like that.

"An' another thing. 'The Rock' didn't want to take it up. Not with negotiations in progress. So he let it go.

"I mean, what could you do? The man was dead."

"But maybe they could've done something about it. At least it wouldn't happen to the next guy," Davies said. "Right?"

"Oh, that's right enough," Will said. "But that's not how things work around here. You stick around, you'll see a lot of guys get hurt, even die, in the shop. They won't do anything about it. That's the way things work. You're smart, you ought to know that."

"Yeah," Davies said. "I know that. But that's not how it *ought* to be."

"Oh, shit! Everyone knows things aren't the way they *ought* to be. But how you goin' to change that?"

"I don't know," Davies said. "There gotta be a way. It ain't right."

"Well. . ." Will took another deep breath. "I know that." He fell silent.

"But I will tell you one thing," he said. "Barney was one hell of a guy. The day he died, a lot of people, more'n just me, were pretty broke up about it. He was a good ol' guy, Barney. One of the best. A lot of guys goin' to miss him around here."

"For sure," Davies said. "But it's a goddamn crime! . . ."

"That it is," Will answered. "I know it. A goddamn crime."

"We just can't let it end there," Davies said, looking out across the factory floor, a grim expression on his face.

Trouble
on the Hill

1

Shouts and sounds of broken glass jolted Flaherty out of a deep sleep:

"Niggah!"

"Niggah, go home!"

"Move out, niggah! Move out!"

"Don' wan' no niggahs heah!"

He strained to listen, his heart suddenly thumping hard in his chest. Everything was quiet. There was another sound of shattering glass, a window bursting apart, and more shouts:

"Niggah!"

"Niggah, get out!"

Raucous laughter in the street, jeers and whoops. High-pitched voices. Taunts.

"Nig-*gah!*"

He lifted his head to see the bedroom clock. Two-thirty. He was wide awake, adrenalin pumping through his system. He turned to glance at his wife in bed beside him. She was still asleep, one arm flung across her face, her mouth half-open. Quietly, so as not to wake her, he sat up and swung his legs over the side of the bed, then stood up, smoothing the covers back down so she wouldn't get a draft. He rubbed his face. The noises from across the street continued.

He put his slippers on and, lifting his bathrobe off the bedroom chair, walked into the hall and down the stairs, putting his arms through the sleeves and drawing the robe about him as he moved. He went into the living room and drew the curtains.

The streetlights' cold purple glare lit up the scene: a group of five young white men were standing on the lawn facing the house across from him, dressed in blue jeans and lightweight nylon jackets. Two of them were holding bricks. They bent down and whispered among themselves; then stood up, laughing. One hurled his brick against the side of the house, then scurried back towards the street as if afraid of an explosion. He picked up another brick from a small stack there and ran back to the others, wagging his head from side to side, with a comical pop-eyed face.

Two of the youths edged off to one side, looking nervously up and down the street. They motioned to the others to leave.

"This is just a warnin'!"

"Yeah. A warnin'!"

"You jus' get out, niggah. Get out while you still have the chance."

"Or else we'll be back, and not jus' to bust a few windows."

They looked at one another and grinned, pleased with themselves. Two more bricks flew towards the house. One bounced off the side with a crisp *thwack*. The other shattered a window on the first floor, the glass tumbling downward like a skyrocket.

"You heah, niggah, you heah?"

He felt a hand on his shoulder and jumped, then spun around. It was his son, Jimmy.

"Wake you up, too?"

"Uh-huh."

They both looked out the window.

"Hey, ain't that the Wilson kid? Tommy?"

"Looks like him, don't it?"

The youths huddled together for a few seconds, then all turned and started running away from the house, heading down the street to the right, towards the bottom of the hill. Their footsteps resounded through the empty street, their retreating jackets still visible. Then they were gone. The street was quiet again, its walkways and houses and trees unmoving beneath the relentless glare of the purple lights.

A window lit up on the second floor of the house across the way. Then another, to the left. Then one on the first floor.

"Looks like they got a lot of windows broken," Jimmy said.

"I know." Flaherty leaned forward. "I wonder should I go over."

"Why, Dad?"

"I don't know. See if anyone was hurt. They might need help."

"They can take care of themselves, can't they?"

"Maybe." He pulled his bathrobe more tightly around himself. "Hey, you don't have to come."

"I'm going if you are."

"Okay." He was already moving towards the front door. "Let's go."

They walked out together. The October night was cool and damp. A few fallen leaves swirled lazily along the ground, stirred by a western breeze. Was it his imagination, or were they being watched by people hidden behind dark windows in other houses along the street?

They moved across their front yard, crossed the street and approached the house. Splintered glass was all over the lawn and bushes which bordered the building. The living room picture window was shattered, as were a kitchen window and several smaller ones upstairs. Glass littered the driveway, too.

They walked up the path to the house, climbed the three steps and knocked.

No answer.

"Maybe we should go," Jimmy said hesitantly.

Flaherty knocked again. "Hello," he called. "Hello!"

A faced looked down from an upstairs window, then disappeared. He heard footsteps. Someone was coming. A voice: "Yes?"

"It's Flaherty. From across the street."

"Oh." The door opened a crack. "What do you want?" A man's voice, taut and high-pitched, frightened, mistrustful.

"Is everyone all right?"

"Yes, I think so." The door opened further. The man was dressed like himself in pajamas and a bathrobe. He was of medium height, slender, his curly black hair flecked with grey. In his late thirties, Flaherty thought. His voice had a musical Caribbean accent.

"They woke me up," Flaherty said, gesturing awkwardly with his hands.

"Ah.... I see." The Black man was quiet for a moment. "Yes." He tried a smile but couldn't pull it off. "They were a bunch of hoodlums, I think."

"I think I recognized one of them. A neighborhood kid."

"Yes. . . ." He said it like a question.

"Paul?" A woman's voice came from upstairs.

"Yes?"

"Who is it?"

"The man from across the street."

"Flaherty," Flaherty said.

"Mr. Flaherty."

"Oh." There was the sound of walking and a door closing.

"Well . . . ." The man smiled, this time successfully, as if to say he was all right.

Flaherty nodded. "Okay. I just wondered if you needed anything. I guess you're all right."

"Yes. Thank you for coming over," the man said. Then he sighed, long and heavy, from deep-down. "I think they are gone now. There are a few windows broken, but we can fix them tomorrow. Now, I think, we will try to go back to sleep."

"Okay." He took a step backwards, towards the street. "Well, if there's anything we can do to help. I mean," he waved his hand, "don't get the idea that everyone in the neighborhood is bad just 'cause of a few rotten apples."

"Okay. Thank you for coming over."

Flaherty nodded again. "All right." He backed away, Jimmy at his side. "Good night."

"Good night."

They turned. The door closed behind them. They went down the stairs to the driveway and started back across the street.

Once again, he had the feeling that others were watching from the silent windows of their homes which lined the street.

"Asking for trouble, aren't they?" Jimmy said. "Moving in here like that. There ain't another Black family on the block."

"Maybe. But they got a right to move where they want, don't they? Punks got no business starting trouble. It don't matter what color he is, a man's home is his home."

"Maybe that's true, Dad, but you know how people feel. A lot of 'em don't want any niggers on the street."

"Jimmy," he said sharply.

"All right." He corrected himself, "A lot of 'em don't want any *Black* families on the hill. It's that simple."

They reached their house. "You know what's going to happen," Jimmy went on. "You know this is just the beginning. Really. Kids were talking about it in school today. That's all I'm saying. There's going to be trouble."

He opened the door, and they went in. Flaherty took a deep breath. "Well, that don't make it right," he said. He shook his head. "Anyway, let's go back to sleep for now."

They separated. Flaherty went back up the stairs to his bedroom. His wife, Ellie, was still asleep. He took his robe off and hung it on the chair, then kicked off his slippers. Easing the covers back, he slid into bed without waking her. It was so quiet he could hear the clock ticking. He closed his eyes, but couldn't fall asleep. The clock, his heart pounding. Jimmy was right. This was just the beginning. There was going to be more trouble. There hadn't been any trouble in the neighborhood since he moved in fifteen years ago, but now it was starting.

He kept trying to go to sleep, knowing he had a long day's work coming up, but he tossed and turned for more than an hour. And when he did sleep, his sleep was filled with fitful dreams.

2

The next day passed quickly. Flaherty barely had time to tell Ellie about the incident before he had to leave for work. And at work, though his mind kept returning to the image of the five youths outside the Black man's house, he didn't say anything about it to his friends. Besides, it was one of those days when a bunch of workers called in sick, and he was assigned to extra runs on the city buses he drove. He didn't have time for talking.

When he came home, Ellie was in the kitchen.

"Bob?"

"Yes."

"The whole neighborhood's talking about what happened last night."

"Oh?" He opened the refrigerator and pulled out a cold beer, then closed the door and sat down.

"Most of it's Sharon Darcy's doing. She's been going around telling people the 'niggers' got what they deserved, and they're going to get worse if they don't move out. She says Harry told her if this one family stays, there'll soon be others, and then the value of everybody's house will go down, and. . . ."

"Oh, Jesus!" He exclaimed. "How many times have I heard that talk before!"

"Some of it's true, though, isn't it?"

He waved his hand. "Aaah. Not really. Not unless everyone panics all at once. Hey, we're only talking about one family here. Not an immigration."

She nodded. "Anyway, Sharon's been going all around, telling people this. She's gotten a bunch of people all steamed up."

"Like who?"

"I don't know. Sally Brock. Kelly."

He leaned back from the table, rubbing his forehead. "That Sharon's always looking to make trouble for someone."

"I know."

"No one around here's going to take what she says serious."

"Maybe not. But a lot of people *do* feel something's going to happen." Her voice held a note of anxiety.

"For sure. You can bet on it. Something else *is* going to happen. Whoever started this won't stop with a few rocks." He took a panatella out of his pocket, tore off the cellophane wrapper, and stuck the cigar in his mouth. "You got a couple bad elements here, same as anywhere else." He reached for his lighter. "Gives the rest of us a bad name." He lit the cigar, sending up a thick cloud of shiny blue smoke, then leaned back and took a couple of deep puffs.

Ellie was quiet for a moment. "Sharon's been telling people you went over there last night."

"So?"

"Nothing. I just thought you'd want to know." She picked an imaginary crumb off the table and threw it away.

He looked at her, waiting to hear more, but she didn't say anything. "Okay. So now I know. What else?"

"Nothing," she said peevishly. She glanced away, then back at him, then lowered her eyes. "I mean," she paused. "Do you really think it was smart for you to go over there?"

"Smart? I don't know. It was *right.*" He tried to catch her eye. "Do you?"

She kept looking down at the table. "I don't know. It's just that people are talking about it. . . ."

"Ellie," he said. "Look at me. Do you think it was wrong of me to go over last night and see if I could help out? Do you?"

She glanced up at him, then looked away. "No, I guess not." She flicked imaginary crumbs off her dress. "I just don't want us to get mixed up in all this, that's all." She suddenly stood up and began clearing the table, putting dirty dishes in the sink, emptying the ashtray, straightening the salt and pepper shakers.

"Ellie, I don't want you getting upset about it."

"I'm not upset!"

"I don't want us to get in any trouble, either. I was just trying to help."

"It's just that people *talk!*" she cried.

He kept his voice low and controlled. "Let them talk. Hey! No one listens to Sharon Darcy anyway. Believe me."

She sighed, then sat down. "All right. I'm sorry." She leaned over towards the stove and turned the kettle on. "I think I'll have a cup of tea."

"Okay." He reached out and patted her arm, sliding his hand down over hers and letting it rest there for a minute. Then he stood up, crossed to the refrigerator and got himself another beer. "Jeez, it was a hard day at work. Half the crew's out sick. I didn't have a minute." He sat down again and opened the beer, took a swallow.

He could hear the sounds of kids playing outside; an airplane overhead.

He glanced at Ellie. She was looking at the kettle on the stove. He noticed how gaunt her hands were and remembered that they hadn't always been that way. They'd been thin, but not as tight and bony as they were now. Her face was thin, too, with deep lines around her eyes. Ellie had worked hard. She'd borne four children and lost another, raised the kids while he worked two jobs; and then, when he dropped his other job, she'd worked for three years in the shoe factory. Now she was home again. They'd almost paid off the house. But it hadn't been an easy life for either of them, to make it as far as they had now.

He puffed his panatella reflectively, enjoying the moment of calm.

When the water boiled, Ellie stood up and made herself a cup of tea. "Bob," she said. "Why do people get so steamed up because this family's moving in? Honest. They seem like hard-working people, decent folks." She shook her head. "I don't know. People get so worried. . . ."

"I don't know. You hear all sorts of stories. Some people expect the worst."

"You've never been like that."

"No. But you got to remember, I grew up in Roxbury, in the days when it was a changing neighborhood. The old days. And my old man, he was a real fighter against prejudice. I think it was tied up with him being so active in the union, being on strike a couple times, and learning to stick together with all the workers, whether they were Black or white. You know? So I grew up seeing people just as people. I can't remember ever looking down on Black people just because they were Black. To me, if you're a good Joe, then you're a good Joe, white or Black.

And if you're a bastard, then that's it, whatever color you are."

"I guess that's true."

"It is."

"But feelings sure run high the other way."

"Of course they do," he said. "Like at work, some guys think that way. That the Blacks are after their jobs, their homes their wives, their daughters, whatever." He gestured. "But I'll tell you one thing. When it comes to getting a better contract with the city, even these guys will work hand in hand with the Black workers. They know it's the only way they'll ever win anything."

"Uh-huh." She sipped her tea, quiet for a moment. Then she said, "I found out some more about this Black family."

"Oh?"

"They're not American Black people. They're from Haiti."

"I *knew* he had some kind of accent."

"His name is LaCouture. Paul LaCouture." She leaned forward, eager to share the information she'd found during the day. "He works in the bakery down Warren Avenue. His wife's name is Jacqueline. I think she works at City Hospital."

He nodded, puffing his cigar. "Like you say, hard-working people."

"Really. They've got five children. The oldest is going to college somewhere. Then there's two girls in high school. And a boy who goes to the same school as Karen, as it turns out. And a little boy, couldn't be more than about three. Some woman comes by in the morning and helps take care of him. Kelly says she heard they got burned out of another home somewhere, but that's only a rumor."

"Uh-huh."

She lit up a cigarette. "That's what I heard."

"Well," he yawned, then stood up, "I'm sure there's more to come from all this." He turned towards the front of the house. Through the living room window, he could see the LaCouture's house across the way, a snug one-family home two stories high, with a steep arched roof and gables poking out in all directions. It had new green vinyl siding, and the front walkway was lined with hedges. The picture window had been taped up.

He tapped his cigar ash into the ashtray on the kitchen table, then jammed the stump back in his mouth and started towards the living room. "Think I'll just walk around a little," he said.

"Okay. I'm going to start supper."

He walked into the living room, then turned and went out the front door and stood on the porch. He looked around.

It was a neighborhood on a hill. The streets wound in elliptical bands, with names like Bradford and Pembroke, rising steeply in some places and remaining fairly level in others. A church was up at the steep end of the street, commanding a fine view of the city; and there was a school near the bottom of the hill, where most of the kids went.

For the most part, the homes were one and two-family dwellings built around 1900. Though none of them were elegant now, the neighborhood had been considered well-to-do in the early part of the century. Now it was inhabited by working people, trying their best to keep it up. Some of the homes were like mansions, sprawling in all directions at once. But most of them were simpler, two or two and a half stories following a Gothic line, with gables and dormers, porches and modest front lawns, and were painted different colors—deep blue, white yellow, dark-brown.

Behind the houses, reaching higher on the hill, were some clumps of trees. But most of the hill had been carved into small lots, and there the trees were confined to a few backyards and occasional spots on the sidewalk.

Being on a hill, they had a good view. The center of the city lay to the north. Off to the south they could see the giant silver storage tanks of the gas company, a reservoir, a bay where people went swimming on hot summer days, the expressway stretching off to the southeast and the suburbs, the railroad tracks, the subway, which was aboveground at this point, adjacent to the railroad tracks heading to New York City. Far off to the east, on a clear day, they could trace the purplish-green line of the ocean, blending with the blue tones of the sky.

It was an old neighborhood. Mostly Irish, but with some Italians and Greeks, and a few Poles. These nationalities were already two generations mingled into America. The men worked for the electric company, the gas company, in construction, in hospitals, in factories, driving trucks, in department stores. Some were laid off. As a rule, the women worked too, in small stores or in the downtown stores and hospitals, as well as the shoe and garment factories. A couple of families had no one working, and were living off savings and welfare, unemployment checks, food stamps and whatever they could get from relatives. But mostly people were working.

He could feel the neighborhood trying to maintain itself, trying to keep up a good front in face of rising costs and changes. Some of the houses had begun to deteriorate. They needed a new paint job, a window or two, new stairs or support for a sagging porch. Some people had had trouble getting loans for home repairs. That was a bad sign.

The people, like the homes, were facing tough times. Folks didn't have much reserve to fall back on, and he knew many who had to "do without" things. The kids "did without" dental checkups. The grownups "did without" a new car. The houses "did without" new roofing. It was not a poor neighborhood, but it was a neighborhood in transition. When they could, families like the Oldhams bought new one-family homes on clean flat streets in suburbs like Dedham, Quincy or Norwood, where there weren't so many two and three story homes, and where everything was white and neat. The ones who stayed on the hill were the ones who had to stay.

A bunch of kids were playing on the street, Jimmy among them. Someone's cat was on a front porch, warming itself in the southern sun. A teenager swerved down the street on a skateboard, a terrier chasing him, yapping at the rollers. People like himself were coming home from work.

It was a quiet neighborhood, he reflected. He'd lived there with Ellie and the kids for fifteen years. He'd seen his kids grow up there, play in the streets, explore the top of the hill and the beach at the bottom, get confirmed in the church, hike down to the playground. . . .Was all this going to change now? Just because a family named LaCouture instead of Hallihan or Moretti had bought the two-story home from old Heywood.

How could anybody be threatened by that?

The sunny afternoon was one of the last days of Indian

summer. After this it would get chillier. But, damned if he was wrong, he felt something in the air besides the fragrance of yellowing leaves and the smells of early dinners cooking. There was a slight hush, a stillness, a sense of people watching more than usual, watching and waiting as if they were holding their breath. . . .

"Bob!"

He turned and went back into the house.

3

Nothing happened that evening, not the next night, either. But Flaherty felt it was just a matter of time.

"There's guys coming to school and hanging out in the bars and on the street," Jimmy told him. "Not even from our neighborhood. I think they're from South Boston. Trying to get the kids to do something."

"Like what?"

"They don't say. They just talk a lot about how if 'one' moves in, 'another' will be right behind, and how you have to fight it and 'keep the niggers' in their place. A lot of talk."

"What do your friends say?"

"Most of the guys I know don't want the Black family in here. But they don't want any trouble, either. Some guys, sure, they're up for doing something."

Flaherty nodded.

"It's funny," Jimmy went on, "but they don't like the idea of people from some other part of the city coming here and telling us what to do. They want to handle it their own way."

On Friday morning, Flaherty glanced out the living room window on his way to the kitchen. Large uneven black letters were spray-painted across the front of LaCouture's house: **NIGGER, GET OUT.** The Haitian was already outside with his wife and two daughters, trying to wash the letters off with soap and water.

Flaherty talked about this with his friend Will at work.

"It's like a game of cat and mouse," he said. "Tension all over the neighborhood. You know these people are going to bed every night expecting to be waked up."

"It ain't the first time," Will observed.

"I hear they're getting phone calls now, too."

"Hey. This just happened last month somewhere in Hyde Park. Same thing. Family moved in, stayed a week, got all their windows busted, moved out."

"At first I thought it was just kids. But now, I don't know."

"It ain't just kids," Will said. "They got their whole thing organized. Your kid's right. It's these hardcore nuts from South Boston. Except they got some other people going along with them."

Flaherty shook his head. "Maybe. But this time it's right across the street from where I live. I don't like it."

"But what're you going to do? You don't even know who you got to deal with."

They came Saturday night. Loud shouts woke him up at 3:00 a.m.:

"Niggah. Niggah. Niggah, get out!"

"Get out while you can."

He got out of bed quickly and put on his pants.

"Where are you going?" Ellie said.

"Downstairs."

He went to the living room window again. There were about fifteen people in front of LaCouture's house. Some of them in a bunch, chanting and waving their arms; others gathered on the front lawn, setting a cross on fire. One or two of them were wrapped in white robes, with tall peaked hoods.

Jimmy joined him at the window. So did Karen. He could hear Ellie getting up, too. People were probably up all over the neighborhood.

"What's going to happen, Dad?" Jimmy asked, his voice in his throat.

"I don't know."

"What're they going to do?"

He gritted his teeth and shrugged. Across the way, the cross went up in flames, like a burning scarecrow. The fire lit up the whole area, casting yellow and orange shimmering shadows across the sides of the house. Spurred on by this, the crowd whooped and shouted. Some of them began dancing in front of the cross. He saw several of them with bottles of beer.

"NIGGAH!" they shouted. "GET OUT, NIGGAH, GET OUT, NIGGAH, GET OUT!"

Others took up the chant, clapping their hands, dancing, laughing, parading about. "GET OUT, NIGGAH, GET OUT! GET OUT, NIGGAH, GET OUT!"

"You recognize anybody?" Flaherty said.

"Not really. A few yes. But most of them are strangers to me."

"Like they don't come from around here."

"Uh-huh."

"I only recognize about two or three, too, and I've been around here for fifteen years."

"What's happening?" Ellie asked. She had come down from the bedroom and now stood next to them, wiping the sleep from her eyes.

"You can see for yourself," Flaherty said.

"If they'd just move out, this kind of thing wouldn't have to happen," Karen said.

"That's not the point," Flaherty snapped, suddenly feeling very angry.

"If this keeps on, somebody's going to get hurt," Ellie said.

"I know." He paced about in front of the window. "I'm going to call the cops. Maybe they can cool things out." He crossed to the hallway phone and dialed the police number. It rang for a long time before someone answered.

"Twelfth Precinct. Sergeant Hayes."

He told the officer what was happening. "If you don't get over here pretty soon, there's going to be trouble," he said.

"Okay. I'll tell the boys." The man sounded almost bored. "And what's your name?"

"Flaherty. I live across the street."

"All right, Mr. Flaherty. We'll send a car out."

"Thanks." He hung up the phone and went back into the living room.

The crowd had grown to about twenty now. Most of them stood around in front of the cross, clapping their hands and shouting. The lights from the flames gave their skin a burnished orange tone and emphasized the whites of their eyes and teeth.

The two white robes were parading in front of the crowd, waving their arms, organizing the chants.

A few teenage kids from down the street arrived at the scene and stood at the edge of the crowd watching what was happening, blinking and grimacing.

Suddenly a face appeared at the front door of the house: LaCouture. He began waving his arms, shouting at the crowd. A young slender Black man stood next to him, a grim expression on his face.

The appearance of the two Black men set the crowd in motion. People pressed forward towards them. One or two rocks were hurled at the house, bouncing off the siding near the front door. The organized chanting broke down, and different people began shouting all at once instead:

"Niggah!"

"Why don't you get your ass out of here?"

"Go home!"

"Can't you see you're not wanted?"

LaCouture raised his arms, trying to quiet them down. He gestured again and again, waving his hands palms down, like the wings of a bird in flight.

It did no good. The howling increased, and more stones flew towards the house. A window on the second floor was shattered. One of the stones glanced off LaCouture's head, drawing blood.

"Dad!" Jimmy said, pointing to the side of the house. "Look."

Two youths were trying to set the side of the house on fire with a can of gasoline.

The window above them opened, and a young woman's face appeared, frightened and angry. She shook her arms at them and began shouting. She was about fifteen, in her pajamas.

The youths looked up and laughed. One of them gave her the finger and shouted something up at her. The other dropped to his knees and pulled some matches from his pocket. He lit one and held it against the side of the house. It burst into flames.

LaCouture saw them. He pushed the front door open quickly and came hurtling out, his mouth open and his eyes flashing, his arms beating the air, as if propelled by some superhuman force.

Flaherty's throat tightened. He knew the man, controlled by the instinct to protect his family, was incapable of acting rationally now. This meant he was in danger. "Son of a bitch," he breathed, his pulse quickening.

The Haitian, clad only in slacks and a T-shirt, dashed to the corner of the house. He started beating at the flames with his bare hands. Then he turned and shouted at the two youths. He tried to kick the can of gasoline, but he missed and kicked one of the youths instead.

The front door opened again, and the slender Black youth stood in the doorway. For an instant, he looked at the scene— the burning cross, the crowd, the flickering flames against the side of his house, his father. Then he ran down the steps to join LaCouture.

The fire on the side of the house gasped and started to dwindle, not having fully caught on the siding.

Three other youths approached the building. They were wearing jeans and denim jackets and funny little pork-pie hats. One of them carried a chain.

"Punks," Flaherty muttered.

LaCouture was furious. He was kicking at one of the youths with the gas can. The youth had squared off and was swinging at him.

The approaching threesome shouted at the Haitians, drawing their attention. LaCouture spun around. The one with the chain swung it over his arm in a quick arc. It hit LaCouture squarely across the head. He fell to the ground, blood springing to his face. The younger Haitian screamed and leapt at the youth with the chain, moving to the inside so he couldn't be hit, then ramming his head into the other man's stomach, knocking him to the ground. The youth's two companions fell on top of him, their arms flailing. LaCouture, rising up from where he had fallen, threw himself at the youths with the gas can, his eyes wild, his mouth open.

Suddenly they were all fighting. The three who had just come up had LaCouture's son on the ground and were pounding his head and chest with their fists. LaCouture had knocked down the other two by the side of the house. The son suddenly rolled over and, freeing himself, smashed his knee sharply in one of the attacker's faces. The youth went limp, clutching his face, and then toppled over.

This seemed to infuriate the other two who leapt after the Black youth and tackled him to the ground again. The one with the chain now waved it and brought it down on the young man's body.

Now other people, drawn by the sight of blood and the fighting, came running up. Two more joined in, trying to kick the Haitian as he struggled on the ground.

Everything seemed to be happening in a few instants. . . .

"That's it!" Flaherty grunted, heading for his den.

"Dad!" Jimmy cried.

He took his shotgun off the wall and crammed a handful of shells in his pocket.

"Bob!" Ellie cried. "What are you doing?"

But he was already on his way out. "Leave me alone," he said, pushing her away.

He threw the door open and ran across his front lawn, loading the gun as he ran. Other hands had already picked up the can of gasoline and were pouring it against the side of the house. It would be a matter of seconds before the whole place went up. He saw the faces of the people in the crowd, swollen from too much shouting, glassy-eyed from beer, flushed from the sight of blood.

The cross still blazed furiously on the lawn, bits of rag and shredded cloth dropping from its arm like burning flesh. People were rushing to the side of the house, surrounding LaCouture and his son who were still fighting their attackers. Some of the people brandished clubs.

"Kill the niggah!" one yelled.

And a woman, whose features were twisted into a reddish mask, grotesque in the yellow light, roared her approval: "Kill him! Kill the Black bastard!" her voice hoarse and guttural.

LaCouture's wife was at the second floor window, the fifteen year old girl beside her, both shouting helplessly. Another Black face, wide-eyed, stood next to them: a young boy, his fists banging against the side of the window, his mouth open.

A man dashed past him, his face twisted obscenely. "Kill the fuckin' Black bastard!" he yelled.

Flaherty flipped the safety off. He jammed a shell into the action. There was no time to waste. Perhaps he'd waited too long already. And where were the cops?

He fired into the air.

"All right!" he yelled. "Break it up! That's enough!"

Some people stopped and looked around.

He fired again. "Cool down! All right! That's enough!"

The sound of the shots reverberated through the night. Everyone stopped what they were doing. The youths looked around, fear and confusion on their faces.

"Let 'em loose!" Flaherty shouted.

Dozens of pairs of eyes had turned in his direction, filled with hate.

"You heard me." He pointed the gun at the crowd by the side of the house. "Let 'em loose or somebody's gonna get hurt."

The crowd fell back. LaCouture struggled to his feet. His nose was bleeding, and his mouth and forehead were cut. He had a gash across the side of his face where he'd been hit by the chain. The son stood up, too, pushing people away from him. His face was bruised and swollen. The white youths were also cut and bleeding.

"Niggah lovah!" a woman yelled.

"This ain't none of your business!"

"What the hell do *you* want?"

"We're only teaching the niggah a lesson!"

"That's enough," Flaherty said. "This is kind of getting out of hand, isn't it? Now why don't you people go on back home." He tried to give his voice as firm a sound as he could, keeping the gun pointed at the crowd.

"Niggah lovah!" someone yelled again from the rear of the crowd.

"Shut the fuck up," he said. "Now get moving. You done enough trouble for one night."

The fire at the side of the house had dwindled again and was going out. The Haitians crossed to their front porch and opened the door. "You leave my house alone!" LaCouture shouted. "Go away now!" His teeth glinted in the light. "This is my house. I don't hurt anyone. Nobody should hurt me. No more trouble now." He was breathing rapidly, his eyes on fire, his fists clenched, the blood caked on his face. His voice suddenly rose and he lifted his arm, pointing, glaring fiercely at the crowd. "Because next time, BANG! I take care of myself! Okay?" He stared at them, his eyes passing from one face to the next, his chest heaving, his jaw set. Then he turned and, followed by his son, went into the house. The door closed. People turned back to look at Flaherty who, standing in front of them, was still holding his shotgun pointed at the youths.

A sudden high-pitched wail split the air: police sirens. Two sets of wildly flashing bright blue lights rocketed down the street towards them, preceded by the sirens' scream.

Everyone stood still. The cars screeched to a halt, and two heavy-set officers in blue came running out of each one, guns drawn.

"What's going on?" one barked.

Flaherty stared at them. The crowd of people suddenly sprung to life:

"That man has a gun."

"Fired it twice."

"He could have hurt someone."

"I think he shot me."

"The man's crazy."

"Dangerous."

The woman with the twisted reddish face stepped forward. "Offisuh. This man came runnin' across the street like a madman. Started shootin' his gun. Twice. He coulda hit some of the boys ovah theah."

The officers turned towards him. "You fire that gun?"

"Yeah," he said.

"Okay, buddy. Then why don't you put that gun down."

He swallowed, trying to keep his head clear now. Too much was happening, too quickly. He was really into it now. He cleared his throat. "Officer. These people have been terrorizing this man's house. Look at that cross. They tried to set a fire on the side."

"Jus' trying to teach the niggah a lesson," someone said. And a few people, not many, laughed nervously.

"You just put that gun down. Okay?"

"Are you going to disperse the crowd?"

"I said put the gun down," the officer snapped. "We ain't got all day."

"And the family?"

"We'll take care of things."

He looked around. Two of the officers had their guns trained on him. The Haitians were watching from the upstairs windows. The crowd was starting to stir again.

"Arrest him!"

"That man's dangerous."

"Look," he said. "I live across the street. I saw these people try to burn the house down. Hitting that man," he pointed to LaCouture, "with a chain. Someone was going to get killed!"

"He's right," LaCouture called from the window. "Everything he says is the truth."

"You can't just leave these people standing here!" He felt like he was way out on a limb. Here he was, with a shotgun in his hand, surrounded by dozens of people who were ready to tear him apart, and cops with guns trained on him.

"Okay, buddy," the cop said.

"Arrest the niggah lovah!" someone yelled.

"Officer. I think one of my friends here got wounded."

"Yeah," the friend said, holding his arm up to the crowd. There was blood on it. "The niggah-lovin' bastard shot me."

"That's it, Mac," the cop said, reaching for the muzzle of his gun.

Something inside him snapped, and he panicked. For an instant, he went ice cold, and then a deep-searing flash burst over him and, dropping the gun, he turned and began running desperately towards the other side of the street, towards his house.

"Watch it, Bill!" a cop shouted.

"Look out!"

"Get him!"

Something heavy hit him on top of the head, making him spin. He was opening his mouth to explain, when a fist crashed against his lips, sending a sudden gush of hot sticky liquid against his tongue. He tasted salt.

"That man tried to help me!" he heard the Haitian yelling. "He's done nothing wrong! If it wasn't for him, this house would be on fire now!"

Instinctively, he twisted away, jerking his head back and pulling his fists up. He heard the crowd hooting and chanting.

"Come on," a voice said.

"You're under arrest. . . disturbing the peace. . . firing a loaded weapon. . . assault and battery. . . ." He was being dragged away and shoved into one of the cars.

"Niggah lovah!"

A billy club landed hard against his skull. Something else smashed against his cheek. He sagged. He couldn't see anymore. Something sharp hit his side. Handcuffs snapped on his wrists. He lurched forward into the blackness.

4

The next few hours were hard for him to recall. Things were all jumbled together. He remembered being awakened by someone slapping him with a cold towel. Then faces looking down at him, faces and blue uniforms. He was aching all over, his face like a punching bag, his head throbbing. Then the handcuffs coming off. Being dragged in front of some officer to be booked. Jokes made about him by the cops standing around. Looking for a familiar face. Finally seeing Ellie, looking very pale and scared, and Jimmy and Karen, and his cousin Frank who was a lawyer, all dressed up in a suit at 4:00 A.M. Nodding at them but not being able to talk. Being dragged into a back room, then into a cell which was damp and drafty. Then waiting, half dozing off, half awake, the back of his head throbbing, pains in his back and legs. Images from the night jerking their way through his mind—the youths with the gasoline can, LaCouture hurtling towards them from the front door, the faces at the upstairs window, the cross in flames on the front lawn, the report of his gun and the way faces turned towards him, the crowd's chanting. Somewhere in the middle of it, being dragged off again, photographed, fingerprinted, a cup of black coffee being shoved at him, bitter, then back in his cell. He didn't know how much time had passed, but he waited to get out. And, gradually, his mind began to clear and to focus itself. The pains all found specific places to throb from. He grew more alert. He could go over the sequence of events in his mind and start sorting things out. Questions formed, like how come the cops took so long to arrive. He started getting very angry.

Then, suddenly, he was being released. Ellie and his cousin had arranged bail. Two cops brought him from the cell into the front room and gave him his things.

"You can go," they said.

One of the other cops handed him a piece of paper and said something about a date for a hearing.

"Don't worry about that," his cousin   Frank said. "I'll take care of it."

They escorted him outside. It was about nine in the morning and very bright. He blinked.

"Oh, Bob," Ellie said, shaking her head from side to side. "Are you all right?"

"I'm okay."

"Bob. . . ."

"I think I got roughed up a little. What do you say, Frankie? I'm still punchy."

"You look like you were in a scrap," the lawyer said. "They already told us that they had to 'subdue' you."

"They said you were resisting arrest," Ellie said. She started to cry. "Oh, Bob . . . you look awful!"

"I want to bring charges against them. Can I do that?"

"For what?"

"How do I know? For anything. For everything. False arrest, constitutional rights, roughing me up. . . ."

"If you want, we can try."

"I do want."

They drove in Frank's car to the house.

"Did things calm down after they arrested me?"

"Yes," Ellie said. "Everyone went home."

"What's this all about?" Frank asked. "Did you really fire that gun?"

"I guess I did."

"Did you wound one of those kids?"

He bristled. "No way! Those little punks want to stick something serious on me. I shot in the air."

"What I don't understand is why you went out in the first place. It's none of your business, is it?"

He felt exhausted, but his mind was racing. "I don't know. Is it? I just didn't want to see those folks hurt. That's all."

Frank look dismayed, puzzled. He licked his lips and concentrated on driving. "Okay. Whatever you say."

When they reached his house, he looked across the street. It was quiet. The cross was burned down, a charred skeleton on the lawn. The house had a black, blistered area where the fire had been set. Several more windows were broken. The NIGGER GO HOME writing, though somewhat soaped away, was still legible across the white front of the building.

"Do you want to get some sleep?" Ellie asked.

"I don't know. Maybe I'll try. I want to get a shower first."

"Okay. I'm going to go home," Frank said. "I'll get in touch with you tomorrow. We can talk this whole thing over then." He held out his hand.

"Okay, Frankie. Thanks a lot. For everything." They shook hands, and Frank drove away. Flaherty turned and walked into the house. "Are you hungry? I can make some breakfast," Ellie said.

"That's a good idea."

He said hello to Jimmy and Karen who both looked very worried and then went upstairs to his room. He took out some clean clothes and brought them into the bathroom. He thought he'd shave first, then shower.

Seeing his face in the mirror was a jolt. It looked like a battlefield. His lip was cracked. His right eye was bruised. His cheek was all swollen. "Son of a bitch," he breathed. "They really did a number on me."

He finished shaving and took his shower. It made him tired.

Instead of getting dressed, he just put on his bathrobe and went downstairs for some coffee, toast and eggs. Nobody had much to say. He felt they wanted to talk but didn't know how to go about it. After eating he announced that he was going to try and get some rest, and he left the table, climbed the stairs to his bedroom again, pulled the covers back and climbed in, drew the covers over his head, and was soon asleep.

He awoke late in the afternoon. When he went downstairs, the whole family was there. Not just Jimmy and Karen, but his daughter Marian and her husband Ken also.

"You must have been one hell of a wild man," Ken said, grinning at him. "Jesus!"

"How're you feeling, Dad?" Jimmy asked.

"I'm okay," he said. "What's the big occasion?"

"I asked Ken and Marian over for dinner," Ellie said. "And I thought we should all talk about what happened."

He sat down in his favorite chair. "Okay. What's on everybody's mind?"

"Dad," Marian said. "Maybe you didn't hear it, but the phone has been ringing all afternoon."

"We had to take it off the hook," Ken said.

"Just crank calls," said Ellie. "You answer the phone and they hang up. Or they say something nasty and then hang up."

Flaherty didn't say anything. Ken and Marian, on the sofa next to each other, were leaning forward. Ken had his serious face on.

"Anyway," Marian said. "We took the phone off the hook. Ma's all upset over it. And Jimmy went outside to play with his friends and some of the guys started on him being a nigger lover and all."

"News travels pretty quick," he said.

"It's not funny, Bob!" Ellie cried. "The kids and I have to live in this neighborhood. Whatever you do, we have to deal with the consequences."

"So what are you saying?" His voice had an edge to it.

"I don't know," Ellie said, her voice tremulous. "I *told* you people had strong feelings about all this. But you wouldn't listen. I *asked* you not to get involved, but you had to go out there last night. And now, you've gotten yourself arrested and hurt and this whole thing is blowing up in our faces and. . . ." Tears sprang to her eyes, and she couldn't finish her sentence. She wiped her eyes with the back of her hand, looking away from him, her features twisted into an agonized expression.

"I mean," Ken said, "it's not even your *business* what happens. But you just go off half-cocked, and. . . ."

"Wait a minute," he cried. "Let's get a few things straight here. Okay?" Now he was angry. "What do you want me to do, stand by my window and watch two people get beaten to death, a house get burned down, a bunch of punks tear an innocent family apart? I'm supposed to watch it all happen? Or maybe you want me to lie upstairs in bed with the covers over my head and pretend nothing's happening at all!"

"Dad, that's not what we're saying," Marian said.

"Then what the hell *are* you saying? I mean, *I'm* not the bad guy in all this. I'm sorry if the phone's been ringing, and I'm sorry if people talk, but I didn't go out last night just to make your lives miserable. Okay?"

"Dad, calm down," Karen said.

"Jesus Christ!"

"Dad!"

"And another thing. Who was it called the cops in the first place? Me! But they didn't come, did they? They didn't goddamned come until it was too late, and then the only person they arrested was me. All right? Not one of those punks. Not one of the troublemakers. *I'm* the one gets arrested and beat up. Isn't there something a little funny about that!"

"All right, it *is* a little strange," Ken began, "but. . . ."

"But *what?* That's how it was."

"But you could have really gotten hurt," Marian said. "You could have gotten killed. Who knows what?"

"What she means," Ken added, "is that it's pretty dumb risking your life for a few coons."

"That's maybe *your* opinion," he barked. "I don't happen to share it."

"It is," Ken said loudly. "The way I see it, they're the ones that started all the trouble by moving in here. They knew what this neighborhood was like. They knew they'd be the only Black family. But they went ahead. And now they've got you in a mess, and all of us along with you."

"I guess we see things differently," he said. "We always have. I don't think the family is to blame at all. They got a goddamn right to live where they want without getting a bunch of punks and hooligans on their front lawn!"

"Maybe they got a 'right,' " Ken said. "But this is the real world, and you got to deal with the way things are. There's a lot of people out there who don't want niggers in the neighborhood, and they'll do anything to prevent it."

"I know that."

"So, talking about 'rights' don't make sense. That's all I'm saying, Bob."

"It makes sense to *me*."

"That's not the point. Oh, Jesus, there's no use talking to you."

They were quiet for a minute. Flaherty realized he was breathing heavily, his head pounding. He was trying to make them understand, but he wasn't getting through. They were scared. He couldn't blame them for that. But what did they want him to do?

"I'd do it all over again," he said. "That's how I feel about it."

"I mean, it was a courageous thing Dad did," Jimmy said, in a hesitant voice, as if he was testing the water.

No one responded.

"Well, there you are," Flaherty said. "I guess everybody can't see it the same way now. Maybe we all need a little time to figure things out."

The room was silent again.

"Can I go?" Karen asked. "I got homework to do."

"I guess so," Ellie said. She sighed. Karen stood up and started up to her room. "Dinner'll be ready in about forty-five minutes."

"Okay."

"May as well put the phone back on the hook on your way up," Flaherty said.

"You may have to change your number," Ken said.

"If we have to, we will." He reached for his pack of panatellas. "Want a cigar, Ken?"

"Sure."

He handed him one.

They each unwrapped the cigars and lit them up. Marian turned on the TV. Ken picked up one of the sections of the morning paper and began looking through it.

Ellie stood up. "I guess I ought to see about dinner."

Flaherty followed her into the kitchen. "Ellie."

"What?"

"I just don't want you to get worried about this. We can deal with it. It'll be okay."

"I hope so, Bob." She started getting plates and serving dishes out of the pantry.

"Ellie."

"What?"

"I just got an idea." He paused.

"Well?"

"Dinner don't have to be right away, does it?"

"Why?"

"I want to go over and talk to that family. I'd like it if you came with me."

"Me!"

"You don't have to say anything. Just come. I got an idea. Maybe we can turn this whole thing around."

She hesitated.

"Look. It can't make things any worse, can it? What happened has happened. You can't worry about being involved, because we're already involved. What we got to do now is figure out how to deal with it. Right?"

"You really want me to come?"

"Yes." He put his arm around her. "I want to see how they are, and I want to talk to them about my idea."

"You really want to go ahead with this?"

"Do we have any choice?"

She was thinking it over. "Okay." She gave a funny laugh. "Maybe you're right. If you really want, I'll go with you."

He gave her a squeeze. "Thanks."

"May as well meet these people myself."

"Let's go out the back way. We can tell Ken and Marian later."

They opened the back door and went out together. He was starting to feel better.

5

The street was empty and calm. It was late in the afternoon, a cool clear day without a cloud in the sky. Low in the west, a jet was followed by its pinkish vapor trail, which dissolved a few seconds after being formed. The trees and houses seemed stark in the twilight. There was a smell of ocean in the air.

They went across the street and knocked on the Haitians' door.

"Who is it?"

"Flaherty."

The door opened. "Well. Come in." LaCouture's face was as bruised as his own. He held out his hand. "My friend from across the street. How are you feeling?"

"Not too bad. How about yourself?"

"I'm all right."

"This is my wife, Ellie."

LaCouture held his hand out to her, too. "Paul LaCouture. Come in. Come in." He ushered them into the living room. "Please sit down. Be comfortable. I'll get Jacqueline."

Flaherty sat in an armchair, and Ellie sat on a couch. He looked around. The room was immaculate. He was struck by the appearance of deep red all around him: red and black rug, red velvet couches with matching chairs beside them, heavy red drapes. A gold cupid on the mantelpiece was flanked by old-fashioned shepherd figurines. On an end table next to the couch were photographs of teenagers in graduation dress, interspersed among a group of small china knick-knacks. A small painting of a Haitian peasant scene was on one wall: farmers walking along a road with heavy white sacks on their shoulders, singing. A glass-topped coffee-table stood in front of the couch, decorated with small candy-filled dishes and a set of tiny cups and saucers.

The wallpaper was a heavy white brocade. A gilt-edged mirror was at one end of the living room; and beneath it, on a circular stand, was a vase of bright pink and yellow roses.

LaCouture came back into the room, followed by the woman Flaherty had seen at the second floor window. "This is my wife Jacqueline," he said.

She was a stout broad-faced woman in her late thirties, with brown eyes and straight auburn hair which she wore in a red kerchief. She had on a white blouse and a bright orange skirt.

They stood up to introduce themselves, then all sat down. Flaherty put his hands on his thighs. "Well. . . ." he said.

"I am glad you came over," Jacqueline said. "We appreciate what you did last night. It was the act of a courageous man."

Flaherty nodded, not knowing what to say.

"Are you all right?" she asked.

"Yeah. Just a few bruises here and there. Like your husband. I guess the main problem is going to be dealing with getting arrested, the charges and all."

"But you did nothing wrong."

He grinned. "Tell it to the judge," he said.

"He's been getting crank calls already," Ellie said.

"Oh," said the Haitian. "So have we. Some of these people are determined to make us move out."

"It's got my family pretty upset," Flaherty said. "It's the first time we ever had to deal with anything like this."

"Yes. Well, we have had experiences like this before," LaCouture said. "It's nothing new for us. These people give up when they see they cannot have their way."

"You're not thinking of moving out, then," Flaherty asked.

"No! Of course not!" LaCouture cried. "We have every cent we had tied up in this house. We cannot move. We have to stay. For us, there is no choice."

"But what if the people who came last night don't stop?" Ellie asked. "What then?"

"They will stop. They will *have* to stop. Because I will stay here so long as I am alive. They will have to give in first."

"You cannot be afraid of such people," Jacqueline said. "You cannot always run away."

"I agree with that," Flaherty said. "If you start to run, when're you going to stop?"

"Exactly," she said.

He leaned forward. "Well, one of the reasons I came over here was that I have a plan I wanted to talk to you about. See, I don't think most of the people in this neighborhood are bad. I don't think most of them go along with what happened last night. I've known some of these folks for years. They're decent hardworking people, just like you and me. But I'll say this. And my wife can say if I'm wrong or not. I think a lot of the people here are scared. Isn't that so, Ellie?"

She nodded her head. "That's true."

"A lot of people are scared to stand up for what they believe. I mean, they're afraid to stand up alone. But I think they *will* stand up together. Anyway, that's what I want to find out. I want to go to the neighbors along the block, talk to them and see how they feel. My bet is that very few of them are like this woman Sharon Darcy, what you'd call a hardcore bigot. But if we don't get around and talk to people, then everyone'll sit at home by themselves, upset at what's happening but not knowing what to do about it, and thinking they're the only people who feel that way. Do you know what I mean?"

"I know. I know." LaCouture said, a chuckle in his voice.

"So you want to go around and talk to the neighbors," Ellie said. "What if people think you're a troublemaker. What if you're wrong, and people do feel strongly about this new family moving in? What then?"

"What then?" Flaherty said. "Could it be any worse than it is now, *without* talking to the neighbors?"

"No. Your husband is right," Jacqueline said. "I think he has a good idea. It would find out, also, just who we are up against. Is it just a few people who are causing all this trouble, or do they have a lot of backing?"

"Right," Flaherty said. "We'd be able to find out what we're really up against and not be stuck with rumor after rumor."

"Yes," Jacqueline said. Then she suddenly put her hands to her face. "Oh, excuse me! We are bad hosts. Can I get you both some coffee while we talk?"

They looked at one another. "Sure."

She got up and hurried into the kitchen.

"I'll tell you," LaCouture said. "You and I are strangers. Right? We did not even know one another until twenty-four hours ago. Now we are sitting together in my living room, talking about very important things. This is very good. It makes me certain we were right to move here."

"And you're not afraid?" Ellie asked.

"Afraid? *Of course* I'm afraid," he answered. "I don't want my house to be burned down. I don't want my wife or my children to get hurt. I don't enjoy what happened last night." He rubbed his swollen face. "I don't want it to happen again." Then he shrugged. "But what good is it to be afraid? You have to fight for your rights. That's all you can do. I'm sure many people who stand up for their rights are afraid, but they stand up, all the same."

His wife came back with a wooden lacquered tray, on which was a pot of strong fragrant coffee and four small cups and saucers, sugar and a pitcher of milk. She set it on the coffee table in front of them. They held their conversation until she had poured cups for each of them.

"You know, Mr. Flaherty. . . ."

"Bob."

"You know, Bob," she said, "for us, life has always been struggle. I don't know if you know it, but in our country, the people are poor. Poor farmers and working people. We have a dictator, who rules the people with an iron hand, and the terror of his police." She clenched her fist. "People who speak up are beaten, arrested and tortured. Some are killed. Some of Paul's family were killed in Haiti."

"You can be beaten just for trying to organize a union," LaCouture said. "You can be arrested just because someone tells someone else a comment you made about Duvalier."

"That is why we left Haiti," his wife went on. "It was no longer safe for us. Others leave every day for Canada, Europe. Anywhere they can go."

"I knew about some of this," Flaherty said. "But not about. . . ."

"To leave the country is already a great risk," she continued, her voice growing tremulous. "For example, I left one night, in a small fishing boat, with three other people. This was many years ago, but I can see it as if it was today. I was eighteen years old. We had just been married. We stole out from the village and boarded this tiny boat. If we were caught, it would mean being put in jail. But we were not caught. We did escape. First to Florida, then to New York, and finally here." She leaned back and took a sip of her coffee. "And do you think the struggles stopped just because we had come here safely? Not at all. There was struggle to find a job. Struggle to find an apartment. Struggle to have a good school for the children. So I can say to you, we are *used* to struggle. And that is why we are going to stay on Roscomb Street. No matter *what* these gangs of hoodlums try to do." She took another sip of her coffee, then put the cup down on its saucer on the coffee table.

Flaherty shook his head. "Well. It's true. If you want anything in this world, you got to stand up and fight for it." He was quiet. For a moment, his mind flashed back on his own growing up. The tenements. Fights with the Italian kids on the block. His gang. Being in the Army in Korea. Trying to find a job when he came back. Trying to support his family when the kids were young. Being laid off, recalled, laid off again. Knocking around. Working another job. Working two jobs. Finally landing the job at the MBTA, some security at last. But the fight continuing: over pay, working conditions, the contract. "I guess I know what you're talking about," he said. "Maybe my life's been different from yours, but I still had to struggle every day, just to keep my head above water."

"That's the way it is," LaCouture said. "Struggle every day. You have to fight for what you believe in."

They were quiet for a moment.

"Well," Flaherty said. "So what do you folks think of my idea? Are you ready to start visiting people tonight?"

"I like your idea," LaCouture said. "I will do my share."

"I'll go along, too," Jacqueline said enthusiastically.

"Ellie?" Flaherty asked. "How do you feel now?"

"Better," she said. She turned towards Jacqueline. "I got

pretty upset when this whole thing started. You know, there's been a lot of talk in the neighborhood. . . ."

"You worry what people will think," Jacqueline said, smiling. "I know. I know."

"I think I understand things better."

"Then you want to come with us?" asked Flaherty.

"Uh-huh," she nodded.

"Great!"

"If we don't stand up to whatever this is," Ellie said, "it'll just keep on growing." She reached out and grasped Jacqueline's hand. "I think you're courageous people, too. You knew you'd be in for some trouble when you moved in. But you were willing to face it."

"That's right," LaCouture said.

"Well, I'll go visiting people with you. After all, if Sharon Darcy can go around from door to door, I guess I can too."

"All right!" Flaherty said. "Now we're starting to move!"

6

They visited four families that night, the two neighbors on either side of their homes. At first, everyone had been uneasy; but after a while, they loosened up. All of them were concerned, in their own way, about what had happened.

Stan and Dolly Ramsey told them about their own situation.

"We got two teenage boys of our own," Dolly said. "I'm worried about the gangs going through the streets. They stand outside the bars and the pizza places. They drink in the alleys. Then they get drunk and throw their bottles all over the place, go off and steal cars, take people's pocketbooks and wallets." She shook her head. "I get scared to go out alone after nine or ten."

"But, hey, what can you say?" Stan put in. "These kids ain't got any jobs. What're they going to do? I know a good many of them. My boys know most of them. They come from good families. A lot of them, I know, have been trying to find a job. But they can't turn anything up. So what do they do? Hang out. Join the Army."

"I don't blame the kids," Dolly said. "Like Stan says, most of them come from good homes. But it's getting out of hand."

"And that's who you've got running wild in the streets last night," Stan said.

"Jimmy tells me," Flaherty said, "whoever's doing this has been trying to get these young people to do their dirty work. Like the first night, when those five kids came to throw rocks at Paul's house."

"Sure!"

"They tell the kids that the Black people coming in their neighborhood are to blame for all their problems."

"They are *using* these kids," LaCouture said.

"I know. I know." Stan said. "There's more to this than meets the eye. But the other part of it is, I think it *is* true: the way things are going for these kids, they see a lot of jobs going to minorities when they themselves can't get any."

"These affirmative action programs and all," Dolly said.

"That's what builds up resentment against the Spanish, the Blacks. They see these people getting what they don't have themselves. I think it's a real problem," Stan said.

"That is fine to say," LaCouture said quietly. "But the fact is, unemployment is higher among Black people and the foreign-born than among white Americans. It's always been that way in this country."

"But. . . ."

"So if you see a few programs for hiring minorities, you have to ask yourself why. Why is it necessasy to create special programs? The answer is, people like me have been kept out of many industries for a long time. Like construction work, or firemen. How can that be taking jobs from white people? Shouldn't there be jobs for all in a country as rich as this one?"

Stan shook his head. "Well, I understand what you're trying to say. Maybe it's true, and maybe it ain't. I don't know."

"I think there's things going on we don't have any idea of," Dolly said.

"This is just the tip of the iceberg."

"One thing I agree with," Stan said. "There just ain't enough jobs for everyone who wants them. I seen this at the shipyard. Layoffs. Then they speed everyone up. Then people get hurt."

He paused. "But everything's got another side, and the other side of that is a lot of people get pretty burned up because some of 'em *don't* want to work and are making out like bandits with welfare, unemployment, all that. That ain't fair either."

"So, what are you trying to say?" Flaherty asked him.

"Bobby, I don't know," he said exasperatedly. "I don't know what the hell is going on. And if I don't know, then how do you think those kids feel?"

Flaherty nodded. "Mmmm. That's why we can't let this stuff go on."

"Do you think we have a right to change this neighborhood by moving into it?" Jacqueline asked, her eyebrows slightly raised.

The Ramseys looked at one another for a moment. "Well, I for one *do*," Dolly said. "I ain't prejudiced. I don't care if you are black, white, brown, yellow, green or what. So long as you're a decent person, you got a right to be in this neighborhood. I mean, if a *Martian* wanted to buy a house here, I'd say, fine. But some people are prejudiced, let's be honest about it, and they're the ones that talk the loudest."

"People get scared. That's the truth," Stan said. "Nobody wants to stand out on a limb by themselves."

"Do you know what I can't understand?" Flaherty asked. "It's why so many people are scared. Pete and Sally Brock said almost the same thing tonight as you two. They don't like what happened last night. They don't like what the cops did to me. They don't think Paul and Jacqueline should have to worry about their house being attacked, just because they move into this neighborhood."

"So what are you driving at?"

"Just that," he said. "Okay, Sharon Darcy and a few others want to keep the hill white, no matter what. Most people don't feel that way. So why are so many people scared?"

"Folks don't want to get involved?"

"Is that it? I don't know. Do people think they can just stick their heads in the sand, and everything upsetting will go away?"

"I don't know," Stan said. "I haven't thought about it that much."

The DiRoglimos, Hal and Vera, were polite to the four of them, but standoffish. Flaherty felt they wouldn't commit themselves to anything, and he saw, by the way Vera looked at Jacqueline LaCouture, that she was not at all used to having any social contact with Black people. Her look was a mixture of distaste, curiosity and fear.

"What are you trying to do, Bobby?" Hal asked.

"I'm trying to figure this thing out," he answered. "The only way I can, is to see how other people add it up, too."

"Well," Vera said cautiously, giving Jacqueline another of those looks. "We certainly don't want a riot in the neighborhood. We're against that kind of violence."

"Uh-huh."

"But you were asking for trouble, weren't you, Bobby, when you went out with a shotgun," Hal said. "Isn't that true?"

"Maybe," Flaherty responded, "but here you had a bunch of punks trying to burn this man's house down, smashing people over the head with chains, screaming and yelling. What do you think? Somebody had to stop it."

"Sometimes," LaCouture observed, "you have to fight fire with fire."

"Well," Hal said, moving about in his chair. "That's true. I don't think the cops should have treated you the way they did, Bobby. Now that's one thing."

"For sure."

"I don't know. This whole thing has kind of thrown us all for a loop. Who'd have figured it could have happened in *our* neighborhood. You know what I mean?"

"You mean me moving in?" LaCouture said.

"Sure," Hal said. "You moving in. People throwing rocks. What happened last night. Bobby here with a shotgun. It's all too much, too fast."

"I know," Flaherty said. "That's why we're here."

He tried to put it together afterwards. It struck him, a lot of people figured they weren't prejudiced, that it was the "other" guy. But no one really knew who this other guy was, or what he really felt. They just assumed it. And no one wanted to make waves.

He realized there was a lot more work ahead of them before his plan would move ahead. Talk to more of the neighbors. Figure out how many people were trying to scare the La-Coutures out and how many could be organized to fight against it. It meant getting some support you could see in the community. And also fighting his own case against the cops, because they'd be throwing the book at him.

People would speak out in their own homes against what was happening, but none of the four families he'd seen that night would go out with them, door to door, and help them organize. No one was willing to take a stand in front of his neighbors.

"People are still watching and waiting," he said to himself.

He made plans with the LaCoutures to visit more families the following evening. A few more days would give him a better sense of where things stood. . . .

Home at last, he got himself a beer and sat in the living room, staring at the TV, his body aching all over and his mind on fire. Ellie went to make some tea.

The phone rang. Flaherty grunted, then got up to answer it.

It was a man's voice, loud and hoarse. "You nigger lover," it said. "We're gonna get you, too."

"Aw, go. . . ." Flaherty started to say, but the man hung up before he could answer.

"Who was that?" Ellie called.

"Another crank call."

"Will they go on forever?"

"I don't know. I hope not. Maybe Ken's right, we should get a new number."

"Bob. . . . I know you're doing what you think is right. But, tell me. Do you think these crank calls are serious?"

"I don't know, Ellie. I think they're trying to scare us. It's such a cheap trick, calling up on the phone, then hanging up. Trying to intimidate people like that. That's how a coward does things."

"But someone *is* trying to get us to stop."

"Sure. I guess they are."

"Then they *are* serious."

He sighed. "I guess we have to expect that they are."

She looked at him anxiously. "It's just all happening so fast."

"I know. But look at it this way: we must be doing something right. Otherwise they wouldn't be bothering us."

"I don't think it's funny," she said. "I just wish it didn't have to be us."

"So don't I," he said. "You know I never done things like this before. But here we are. Somebody has to stand up and take the first step. I guess this time it's us."

"I guess."

He sat back and picked up his beer again, lit another panatella, watched the smoke curl upwards. He was being personally attacked now, and he didn't like it. If someone wanted to scrap it out with him, then let him try.

He was going to give it all he had.

7

The Monday morning paper carried a short account of the incident Saturday night, focusing on Flaherty's arrest. Flaherty read it, then threw the paper down in disgust. It made him out to be some kind of nut. It didn't mention how the crowd had been trying to burn the house down. It made the punks seem like a bunch of over-enthusiastic high school kids. And it played the cops up like heroes, preventing further violence. He was furious.

Some of the guys at work had seen the article and tried to kid him about it. But they stopped short when they saw the bruises all over his face. It was clear he wasn't in a joking mood.

A few people asked the details of what happened, and he told them. Stu Sordillo said he was a fool to get beat up for a "bunch of niggers," but others supported what he did.

As the morning wore on, several more workers came up, saying they'd heard about what happened. Some asked if he was hurt. Lew Moran told him he disagreed with what he did and wouldn't have done it himself, but he respected him for having the guts to stand up for what he believed in.

Two of the Black MBTA workers came up to him quietly.

"A lot of people are talking about this," one of them said.

"It's all over the yard."

Flaherty nodded.

"You just take care of yourself," the other said. "Let us know if we can help."

"Thanks," Flaherty said. "I appreciate it."

He had the distinct feeling he was being watched. He knew there were a few hardcore bigots in the yard, and for all he could tell they'd known about the attack on LaCouture's house, maybe before it had happened. He caught a few people looking at him in a funny way, out of the corners of their eyes, as if they were keeping tabs on him.

When coffee break came, he was glad to be able to sit down with his buddies.

Charlie, a curly-haired kid with a long face, went off to get them all coffee and doughnuts. Then they sat down in their usual area. Flaherty lit up one of his panatellas. Al got out his Winstons.

"So what'cha gonna do, Bobby?" Will asked.

He told them. "I'm going around the neighborhood, talking to everyone I can. I want to get to the bottom of this."

"They bringing charges against you?"

"Uh-huh. That's why I figure, if I don't get some support from the other folks in the neighborhood, I'm going to get iced. I don't have any choice."

"Sure. You gotta get other people to back you up," Charlie said. "No doubt about that."

"But you start going out like that, and you're gonna wind up in even hotter water," Al said. He was a balding man about fifty, with small brown eyes stuck in a very round face, like raisins on a snowman. "Once the people behind this find out you're running around trying to organize the block, they'll be after your ass."

He nodded. Al was a good friend. He was a realist, too. Even when they disagreed, he had to take Al's views seriously.

"They already know," he said. "We been getting phone calls. Threats."

"So whattaya gonna do?"

"What *can* we do? Whoever's doing it's a coward anyway."

"I wouldn't be too sure," Will said. "This ain't your usual garden variety punk."

"Whattaya mean?"

"Just, it's more than a bunch of kids. You know what's going on in this city. You read the papers. These guys got a movement going. They beat people up and burn houses, go on marches. All that stuff."

"You think that's who's behind this?"

"Absolutely. It's not a bunch of kids. This is organized from much higher than that."

"Well, maybe I don't know that much about it," he said. "What's all that got to do with me?"

"You got yourself in the middle of it. There's people in the city working hard to get all this racial stuff going."

"Like?"

"Like your real estate people, for one. Driving the whites out because the Blacks are moving in. Get the whites to sell cheap. Then they turn around and sell the houses to the Blacks for a lot more. There's money in that."

"Aw, I don't know if that's so, Will," Charlie said. "Where did you read that?"

"That you got to read between the lines," Will said. "You got to use your eyes and your brain. Check it out."

"You've always got a bad element," Charlie said, waving his doughnut in the air. "But you make it sound like people are doing all this on purpose."

"That's right," Will said. "And I'll bet you something else. There's big money behind it." Will was a lanky French Canadian who'd worked in the lumber mills before coming to Boston. He'd always been something of a radical. Flaherty liked him because he was honest, and because he was always trying to figure out what was "behind" what was happening.

"You take the politicians," Will went on, jabbing his finger at Charlie. "They haven't done a *thing* in this city to get anyone a job, improve the schools, what have you. But now they're all making a stink about busing. You tell me, why are they trying to get everyone fighting each other instead of setting the problems straight?"

"Oh, hell," Charlie said. "Everybody knows the politicians are a bunch of crooked bastards."

"That's right. But you got to look to see where the butter on their bread comes from."

They paused a minute, sipping their coffee and munching on doughnuts. A cool autumn wind was blowing through the yard, and the sun was playing hide-and-seek behind the clouds.

"Well, I don't think Bobby ought to get himself out on a limb," Al said. "I think he ought to be careful."

"Of course," Flaherty said. "But do you think I should just play it cool, quiet down, forget what the cops did to me. . . ."

"Wait a minute. I ain't saying that. Cool down," Al said, grinning at him. "Just, you got to be careful."

"I know. I know," said Flaherty.

"But why'd they move in your neighborhood anyway?" Charlie asked. "Ever ask yourself that?"

"That ain't the point. They just moved. We got to deal with it."

"There's good homes in Mattapan. And cheaper, too. And no trouble there."

"Maybe, but so what?"

"The family's asking for trouble. Am I right or wrong?"

"But that ain't the point," Will said. "Bobby's right. You got to look what's going on all across the city. Why are they making such a stink now? What's it mean?"

Charlie took a deep breath, rubbed his hand on the back of his head. "Maybe. But Bobby's getting himself in a mess over it."

They were quiet for a minute again, each of them thinking. Then Flaherty said what he's been turning over in his mind: "You guys think these people, whoever they are, are too strong for me to take them on?"

"I didn't say that," Al said.

"I think so," Charlie said. "I think you're in over your head."

"Will?"

"I don't know, Bobby," he said. "It's something you got to decide for yourself anyway."

"Uh-huh."

"But you got to think about it," he went on. "You got to respect the kind of organization these people have. Aren't they trying to organize right here, in the yard? Aren't some of them on the Executive Board of the union? You see them bring two, three hundred people out for a march, you know they got their act together."

"Uh-huh."

They looked at one another.

"Will you guys stick beside me?" Flaherty asked. "I'm serious."

"Sure. *We* will," Al said. "But like Will's saying, you got guys in the yard who'd like to see you dead. Right? And maybe hundreds of guys who won't lift a finger. They'll just watch and see what happens."

"Maybe I'll have to talk to the guys in the yard, too," Flaherty said, half to himself.

"Maybe," Will said, "but you can decide that later. Right now, you got to see how things develop."

"Okay," Flaherty said.

"You got a lot of respect in the yard. You know that. You been a fighter here. People aren't going to think you're some kind of nut."

"I know."

"So just see where it goes."

"Okay," Flaherty said. "I will. Thanks."

He thought about it later when he was driving his bus. They weren't just a bunch of punks. There were bigger forces behind it. But it just made him madder. No one was going to treat Bobby Flaherty like that. Christ, his father would turn over in his grave if he thought his son was a coward. And what kind of example would he be setting for Jimmy? A man had to stand by his convictions, and that was that. He wasn't going to stop now.

When he returned home, Ellie met him with a worried look. "The phone hasn't stopped ringing," she said. "A couple of the crank calls. A reporter from the *Globe* wanting an interview. Some people from some group, I forget their name, who wanted to come by and talk."

"I'm not in a mood to talk to anyone," he said, "except the other people in this neighborhood."

"Well, you deal with it, then," she said. "I'm fixing dinner. Oh yes, some of the neighbors have been by, too. I think some of them want to know how you're feeling. Others have heard about what you're doing."

"News travels fast."

"Of course. What about the lawyer?"

"I'm going to call Frank now. I want to get it together. How to fight the charges against me, bring counter-charges. All of it."

"Okay."

"You seem in a pretty good mood."

About a half hour later Jimmy came in: "Hey, Dad," he said. "There's some weird things going on in the street."

"Like what?"

"For one thing, some of the kids were saying that you're a troublemaker. Everybody's talking about it. And I got called a nigger-lover a couple times. Some of the kids wanted to beat me up."

"Did you get in a fight?"

"Not today. But it was pretty heavy for a while."

"Which kids?"

"The ones that always talk nigger-this and nigger-that. They hang out a lot by the drug store. But someone's been giving them drugs. There's suddenly a lot of cheap grass around."

"A lot of kids getting high."

"Uh-huh."

"Figures."

"Dad, I think there's going to be a lot more trouble."

"So do I."

"Are you and Mom still going out tonight?"

"Yep."

"I guess you got to finish what you started."

"Yep. Nobody's going to call our bluff now."

Ellie came into the living room. "What's that?"

They told her what was going on.

"Fine," she said. "Oh God. I guess we're right in the middle of it now."

"Ellie," Flaherty said. "Ellie, babe." He gave her a hug, wrapping his arms, bear-like, around her. "If you ain't got a sense of humor at a time like this, then you're stuck. Right?" He squeezed her like he used to when they were younger.

"Oh, I don't know," she said, pulling away from him, but with affection. "Hey, I got to go fix supper. Karen'll be back soon. And you wanted to go out as soon as we could."

"Okay." He watched her go, then winked at his son. He leaned forward and flipped on the TV, then leaned back in his chair, reaching for a cigar.

8

Three days went by. The phone calls continued, but they didn't bother him. LaCouture was getting them, too, and nothing had happened to either of them. Flaherty kept the reporters and groups away. Very deliberately, he and Ellie and the LaCoutures visited a dozen more families. His hunch was right. Most of the people in the community supported him. Only a very few were hostile.

It was clear that Sharon Darcy and her husband, Winston, who ran a small insurance business down by the Square, had started a lot of the hate talk. Matt Symonds and his wife, Helen, went along with it, too. They were members of the Right-to-Life anti-abortion group that had had a rally in the Common and were known on the block to be pretty conservative.

But the others in the neighborhood didn't go along with them. Art O'Connell, for instance, a construction worker who'd been laid off for four months, said he'd come out any time with Flaherty and LaCouture and stand up to the gangs. He said he was sick and tired of all the nonsense that Blacks were getting this and that at the white people's expense. While politicians were doing a lot of talking, they weren't lifting a finger to help folks out of work like himself. His wife Kelly agreed. She said Sharon Darcy has been all over the neighborhood saying Flaherty was a communist and a troublemaker, but people weren't buying it because they'd known Flaherty for years.

Mary Lester spoke against Sharon, too. She said it was the

first time in two years that Sharon had come to the house, when she wanted to spread rumors about Flaherty. Mary remembered that Sharon had spread a lot of dirt about her and Wally, when he'd been laid off. If anyone was a "troublemaker," she said, it was Sharon and her ambitious husband. Their boy Billy was one of the kids making trouble in school, too.

Wally listened, but he didn't say much. He was working in a laundry now, and he was pretty tired out. He didn't have much use for Blacks, but he didn't have anything against them, either, and he didn't know what all the damn trouble was about, just because this family was moving in.

Pete and Sal Brock, who lived next to Flaherty, told him they'd been hearing a lot of bad talk all through the neighborhood, and they knew where it was coming from. "And not from people who live here," Pete said. He was angry at people he considered rabblerousers, coming into the neighborhood to rile people up. "I mean," he said. "Where'd these people get all the bucks to do what they're doing? Somebody's footing the bill."

Flaherty said that's what his friend from work, Will, had said.

He felt they could win. Maybe the hoodlums could strike at night, when everyone was sleeping. Or make a few phone calls and then hang up. But they didn't have anyone's support. Sure, someone was trying to organize the neighborhood into a little nest of hate, but he had to have confidence in people like himself, the ordinary working people wanted no part of it. Folks were more concerned with putting food on their table and paying the mortgage than with ranting and raving at a Black family that hadn't done a thing to them.

He felt that Jimmy was beginning to enjoy the fight, too. Once the boy had taken a firm stand, he'd found that several of his friends would stick by him. Only a few of the kids were out-and-out punks.

Now if only Karen would come around: she'd been acting like someone else's family was involved, spending a lot of time in her room listening to records, talking to her friends on the phone. He knew Ken and Marian were angry with him for still going around the neighborhood, especially with Ellie; but he didn't think he could change that right away.

The weekend seemed far behind him now. He was more involved with what was coming up than with what had already gone down.

By accident, he ran into the Wilson boy in front of the Star Market. A twinge ran through him, as he recalled the small gang of rock-throwers the night he'd first been waked up. Then he was gripped by curiosity. He wanted to know what made the kid tick.

"Tommy!" he called after him.

The youth kept on walking.

"Tommy!" he called again, hurrying to catch up with him.

The boy wheeled around, a frightened look on his face. He put his hands up to defend himself. "Don't you do nothing to me," he said.

"Hey, I don't want to hit you," Flaherty said. "I just want to talk to you a minute."

Tommy glanced first in one direction, then another, avoiding Flaherty's gaze. "About what?"

"You know about what. About what you were doing in front of my house last week."

"Must be someone else you're thinking of. I wasn't in front of your house. . . ."

"Come on, Tommy! Don't act dumb with me. I saw you out there with the other guys. Throwing rocks and all." He stepped closer to him, lowering his voice. "And I saw you the night I got arrested, too." He paused.

The boy backed away from him and leaned up against the side of the building, still looking away, his chin jutting out pugnaciously.

"Tommy?"

"Whattaya *want* from me!"

"I want to know what the hell you think you're trying to do," Flaherty snapped. "You and your friends."

"Ain't it obvious?"

"You tell me."

"Trying to keep the niggers out. Teach 'em a lesson." He

turned to Flaherty with a sneer. "I guess that's something you don't understand."

"Don't get fresh with me, Tommy."

"Leave me alone, then!" The boy stood in front of him, hemmed in against the wall, a sullen expression on his face.

"Tommy, I know you ain't a bad kid. You used to play games with my Jimmy."

Tommy fidgeted.

"Don't you understand what's going on? Somebody's going to get hurt before all this is over. It's serious."

"I know it's serious," the boy said. "I didn't hurt nobody. You can't say that I did." He tossed his head to get the hair out of his eyes. "You going to tell the cops?"

"No."

The boy sniffed and stood up straighter. "Wouldn't do you any good if you did."

"Oh? How come?"

He shook his head. "Never mind."

"Tommy. Maybe you're getting yourself into something you'll be sorry for later."

The youth snorted a quick laugh. "I could say the same for you, Mr. Flaherty."

Flaherty didn't like the kid being so cocky. "Listen," he said, "I know your dad. Does he know all the things you've been doing?"

Another cocky laugh. "My dad don't give a shit."

"Then why don't we go see him now, you and me, and ask him how come," Flaherty said, reaching out to take the kid's arm.

Tommy yanked his arm away. "Leave me alone! Don't you fuckin' touch me! If I want to talk to my father, then I'll go talk to him. You mind your own fuckin' business!" He moved away, his back sliding against the building. "You let me alone now. I got somewhere I'm going."

Flaherty let him go. "Tommy! You remember what I said," he called.

But the boy didn't answer.

Flaherty watched him walk down the street, feelings of

helplessness and disappointment rising within him.

"Shit," he muttered. He pressed his lips tight together, biting the inner skin. Then he spun to face the other direction, the hill, and began walking.

He had to talk to the boy's father.

The Wilsons lived on Nabnasset Street, just a few blocks from his own house. Gene Wilson worked as a mechanic in one of the auto repair shops nearby. Paula had been involved in church and PTA activities until a few years ago.

They lived on the bottom floor of a green three-story house with a wooden fence around the side, and rows of flowers up the sidewalk.

Flaherty knocked on the door.

Wilson was home. He opened the door, a newspaper in his hand. "Yeah?"

He was a man with a long thin face, prominent jaw, pinched nose, sunken cheeks.

"Hello, Gene."

The man's eyes widened slightly. "Flaherty. What do you want here?"

"Just wanted to talk a minute." He scratched his neck. "Is that okay?"

Wilson grunted. "I guess. What's it about?" He stayed in the doorway, the door half ajar.

"It's about Tommy."

Wilson pulled back slightly, a suspicious look flitting across his face. "What about Tommy?"

"I just ran into him down by the grocery store." He paused. "I wanted to talk to him. He was one of the kids throwing rocks at the house across from mine."

Wilson didn't move an inch.

"I asked him what he thought he was doing, and he gave me some fresh answer. Then I asked if you knew what he was up to, and he said, 'My dad don't give a shit.' "

Wilson's jaws were working up and down, the lean muscles tightening behind the hollows of his cheeks.

"So I said to myself, let's go see Gene and find out if he knows what's going on."

Wilson's jaws kept working. "Uh-huh."

"That's it. I wanted to know what you thought."

He hesitated. "You tell the cops about Tommy?"

"Funny. He asked the same thing. No, I didn't. I got enough trouble with the cops now, or haven't you heard."

"I heard," Wilson said.

Flaherty waited.

"Look," Wilson said, "I don't know what you're up to. I do know you got yourself in a mess of trouble. And as far as I'm concerned, you brought it on yourself."

"Sure, I'm supposed to. . . ."

"You were sticking your nose where it shouldn't have been," he said, raising his voice. "And now, you're doing the same thing again."

Flaherty crossed his arms and leaned back. "I am?"

"Uh-huh. And I don't need you coming here talking about Tommy. You know? You got enough to do, worrying about yourself, and that new nigger friend of yours." He stepped back. "Okay?"

Flaherty looked him square in the face. "So that's how it is."

"That's how it is."

Wilson wasn't angry, and he wasn't scared. He just hated him.

"Suit yourself, Gene," he said, nodding and taking a step back. "Just thought I'd drop by."

"Uh-huh. Well, you did that." He started closing the door. "So long, then."

Flaherty headed home.

His cousin Frankie was waiting for him.

"I've been looking into the law suit you want to file," he said, "against the police. I can go ahead with it, if you want. But I'll tell you right now, it's going to be hard as hell, and you might come out of it in worse trouble than you went into it with."

"How come?" Flaherty asked.

"Because people are talking about it already. I don't know exactly what's going on, but some very important people have been suggesting to me, I guess that's the most polite way of saying it, that you ought to just drop the whole thing. If you drop the suit, then the charges against you might be reduced or even dropped."

"That's a deal, then."

"Call it what you want."

"To hell with it! I got beat up when I didn't do anything wrong. I got a right to satisfaction in the courts."

"All I'm suggesting, Bob, is that the courts might not be inclined to give you that kind of satisfaction, not with the kind of running around the neighborhood you're into now."

"Who's been talking to you?"

"I'd rather not say."

"Shit, Frankie. Are you on my side or not?" He was getting angry.

"Of course, I'm on your side. That's why I'm telling you what's happening. Just be careful. Be careful, Bob. You may be getting in over your head."

"You go ahead and file that suit, Frankie," he said.

"But. . . ."

"And if you don't want to, I'll find someone else. Goddamn it! What the hell's going on around here!" he exclaimed.

"I'm just trying to help you out," Frank said. "I do happen to be a lawyer, and I got some contact with the legal circles in the city, with the courts and the cops, if you want me to spell it out. I can get a sense of how things are shaping up for you. That's all."

"Frankie. . . ."

"Just trying to help. So you don't get hurt again."

Flaherty tried to calm down. "Okay. Okay, Frankie. Thanks. But you got to understand. I'm not getting scared off. I believe what I'm doing is right. Every day, I feel more and more convinced of it. Okay? And this law suit is one way I got of fighting back against what's been done to me."

Frankie opened his mouth, as if to go on arguing. Then he shut it, pressed his lips together and nodded. "Okay, Bob. Let's just leave it the way you want."

"I would appreciate that," Flaherty said. "Hey, things are getting tense around here, Frankie. Don't give me any more problems."

His cousin smiled. "All right. Try to take it easy, then. I'll get back to you later." He headed for the door. "So long, Ellie," he called.

"So long, Frankie."

"I'll catch you later, Frankie."

He opened the door for him and watched him go down the sidewalk to his new Oldsmobile. The lawyer climbed in, started the car up, and drove off, waving to Flaherty at the door. After he left, Flaherty stood by the door for a few minutes, trying to put his finger on what was happening. He'd been successful in his plans so far. But now he was getting the sense that he wasn't the only one with a plan. People he didn't even know were talking about him. Cursing his name. Trying to deal with him.

Frankie knew more than he was saying. Was he trying to *protect* him or what?

The following night he was ripped out of his sleep by an explosion. Ellie bolted up in bed beside him. Flickering lights were coming from outside, and there were bright orange shadows on the wall. He smelled smoke.

They rushed downstairs. It was his car. It was blazing like a bonfire in front of his house.

He called the fire department and told them to hurry, then grabbed his coat and ran outside. Ellie ran out with him, and Jimmy and Karen followed.

The car was completely engulfed in flames.

"Get back!" he said. "Stay away. It might explode."

He stood on the porch, watching helplessly. Flames billowed high in the air. Clouds of thick black smoke spiralled up, high above the houses on Roscomb Street, reaching up towards the top of the hill. The entire neighborhood was lit up.

Fire engines arrived in a few minutes. The firemen hurried about, blocking off the street. Police cars came too. They managed to put the flames out quickly, but his car was a total loss.

Neighbors came to see what had happened. LaCouture and his wife, in their bathrobes. And Pete Brock, Will and Mary

Lester, Art O'Connell, the DiRoglimos, Dolly Ramsey. People gathered in Flaherty's front yard talking excitedly, the charred mass that had once been his car still smouldering.

The fire inspector said someone had broken the side window, splashed gasoline inside the car, poured gasoline underneath it, too, and lit it.

"They want you to stop," LaCouture said. "This is your warning. See, it doesn't matter if you are white or Black to them. They will do to you what they did to me."

"This is more than the work of just a few punks," Pete Brock said.

Art O'Connell was furious. "If they think they're going to scare people with a trick like that, they're *wrong!*" he said. "Maybe some people will back off, but not me. This is *it!* I don't want this kind of thing going on around here any more. Hey! If you need anyone to go around and talk to people with you, I'm ready."

"Let's go inside and talk about this," Flaherty said. "I want to get to the bottom of it. . . ." He was seething. It was all he could do to keep his hands and voice from trembling.

They went into the living room. Ellie made a big pot of coffee.

"The main question I have," Flaherty said, "is whether you folks will stick with us now. Or whether you're scared off."

Mary Lester spoke quickly. "Bob, you don't even have to ask. If they do this to you, they'll do this to anyone. None of us is safe here so long as it goes on. I feel the same way Art does."

"That's right."

"We got to get together and fight this thing."

"We ought to call a community meeting."

"We ought to call the papers and the radio and TV stations and let the whole city know what's going on."

"I'll bet Father Donnelly would help us out." Mary Lester said. "If we talked to him, I think he'd let us have the church for a community meeting."

"That's a good idea."

"I know some groups in the Haitian community that would help us out now," LaCouture said. "Maybe I should have gone to them from the start."

So, at three o'clock in the morning, they mapped out a campaign together. They would divide up all the houses in a four block radius, covering almost half the hill. Two of them would write up a short leaflet, saying what had happened to LaCouture and Flaherty and calling for a community meeting. Mary Lester would talk to Father Donnelly about getting the church. Paul LaCouture would talk to the Haitian groups. Flaherty and Art O'Connell would call up the papers and TV stations. In fact, they'd call up immediately and try to set up some interviews. They would try to get support from the local merchants whose shops were in the Square at the foot of the hill, at least to the extent of putting the leaflet in their windows. They'd talk to the pastor of the Unitarian Church. And everyone would talk to their relatives and friends at work.

By the time they left, they had formed the Roccomb Street Association, with Mary Lester and Flaherty as co-chairmen, and had agreed to meet the following night to coordinate the work.

After they'd gone, Flaherty was so wound up, he couldn't fall asleep. He called reporters, and they came to the house with photographers and interviewed both him and Jacqueline La-Couture.

Suddenly, everything was happening at once.

The next day, Flaherty talked to everyone he could at work about it. He told them to read the evening paper which would have the interview in it. And he invited them all to the community meeting they were going to have that weekend.

Several of them said they'd come. A group of Black workers said they'd be there, with some of their friends.

"We won't let you down," one of them, Harry Johnson, who Flaherty had known for five years, said. "We know what kind of guy you are. And we know what's going on in this city, too."

He sensed that some of the workers were scared to talk to him. He knew some of them thought he deserved what he got, and talked about him when his back was turned. But his close friends, Will and Charlie, rallied behind him, and he found he could get some support from others he didn't know as well, just by going up to them and talking about what he felt.

"Some people heard in advance that your car was going to get hit," Will said.

"I'm not surprised. So, it's not just a bunch of crazy kids."

"No way," Will said. "There's organization behind it. Like I said."

"I guess maybe I been naive," Flaherty said. "But I'm going to get smart in a hurry."

"Let me ask you something," Will said. "Do you want some of us to come and stay at your house? Make sure nothing else happens."

"You mean with guns?"

"If that's what it takes."

He thought it over. "Not now, Will. Thanks. But we should keep it in mind."

He was surprised when Al asked him to go out for a beer with him after work.

"What's on your mind?" he asked, once they'd gotten settled.

"I don't know," Al said. "I guess I'm just curious."

"Yeah?"

"I just want to know why you're doing all this. Why does it matter so much?"

Flaherty grinned. "I'm a strange old bird, huh? You can't figure me out."

"That's kind of true."

Flaherty unwrapped a panatella, lit it, and sucked it reflectively.

"I don't agree with some of this stuff, Bobby. But, Jesus, I got to respect what you're doing." He took a swig of his beer. "I've known you for a long time, and I still don't understand what makes you tick. I just thought. . .well, maybe you could lay it out."

Flaherty grinned again. Al was an old friend. They'd been on the picket lines together. They'd gotten drunk together. They'd gone to each other's children's christenings. He took a deep breath.

"Al," he said, "would it surprise you if I said I don't understand it myself." He paused to wipe his mouth. " 'Cause that's the truth. I don't know what kind of answer you want. I never been against people 'cause of what color they are. Maybe it was the way my father was. I don't know. I remember one time he beat the living hell out of me for calling some guy a 'nigger.' He just didn't believe in those things. But it's probably more than that.

"I mean, when I was growing up, I did play with Black kids. I fought with some of them like hell. Others were my friends. One time, when I was about thirteen, a Black kid named Duke Daniels save me from getting my ass kicked in a fight."

He waved his hands in the air. "But all that is just memory and stuff. It don't explain why I'm doing what I am.

"The only way I can explain it is, that's the way I see things. That's what I've learned from living. That if the Black and white keep fighting each other, none of us is going to get anywhere." He stopped. There wasn't any more he could say.

Al scratched his head. "Well. That's something more than I understood before." He drained his beer.

"Are you going to come to the meeting this weekend?" Flaherty asked.

Al nodded. "Uh-huh. I got to see how this thing turns out," he said.

"Great!" Flaherty said. "I knew you was my buddy."

Now he'd become news. A TV reporter interviewed the whole family on the evening news. The papers had an article on the Roscomb Street Association. Flaherty didn't trust the papers to tell the truth, not after the first article. He thought maybe the violence had "gotten out of hand," and they wanted to put a stop to it.

Father Connelly had agreed to let them use the church on Saturday night. It looked like the tide was turning in his favor.

Even Ken and Marian had called up, worried and apologetic, offering to help.

"I don't agree one bit with niggers moving in," Ken said. "But I'll be goddamned if I'll stand by and see someone in my family attacked in his own home. No sir!"

Karen also pitched in. For the first time, the whole family was united.

Groups in the minority community, prodded by the publicity, called LaCouture and offered to help out. The Association agreed to work with other groups, but they agreed that this was mainly their fight, and they would decide what to do and when, and no one else was going to come in and take things over.

What had begun so small was now a major incident in the city, a test of strength between the gangs and the people on the hill.

9

And suddenly the night was upon them. They'd distributed hundreds of leaflets all over the hill. Over half the shops in the Square had put one up. The papers and TV stations would be sending reporters. Everything was set. They'd gotten enough publicity, and now they had to see how much actual support they had from people in the neighborhood.

Flaherty stood at the door of the church, at the top of the hill. It was almost seven-thirty. The Association had met for dinner at Pete and Sal Brock's house, preparing for the community meeting, and now he was eager for it to begin.

They had tried to organize for all possibilities. It wasn't easy, because none of them had ever done anything like this before. But they helped each other out. Out of all the different ideas, they figured out what was best.

Mary Lester would be chairing the meeting. LaCouture and himself were going to speak about what had happened. Father Connally could be counted on to speak, too. Then they would open the floor for discussion.

The main thing would be having people show up!

He didn't think there would be any disruption. They'd done their work too well. The gangs wouldn't show their face in a well-lit church in front of a lot of people. They'd prefer to go on scaring people in the night, striking while people slept, scurrying about in the shadows. Like cockroaches, he thought. That's what they were like.

They had accomplished a lot in a week. And there was a lot

more to do. But his confidence in the people of the neighborhood had never been broken. It had only gotten stronger. These people, the people who'd lived on the hill for years, the ones whose homes he'd visited, and the people he'd known and talked to at work, they were the backbone of this country. They were the ones who made things move. Once things had been clearly laid out to them and they saw what was happening and why, they could be trusted to do the right thing, come to the right conclusions, take the right steps. Once they were convinced, there was no stopping them.

Already, he'd seen that people could come together. His own family was one example. And the people at work. Sure, he knew it wouldn't be easy, everything didn't happen all at once. But it would happen. He was certain.

That was the task that lay before him. It was as plain as the winding streets and quiet houses that stretched out away from the church, curving down the hill and out of sight to the Square.

The city's skyline was in the distance. A light rain was falling. It was seven-thirty.

Flaherty turned, his heart pounding, and went inside.

Manny

Manny ran a spreader machine, an antique contraption for rubberizing rolls of cloth or paper. He had just finished a roll.

He scraped the stock off the knife, raised the blade and ran the cotton leader through. Then he lifted the roll onto his scale: it was too light.

Either the worker on first shift had put his coats on too thin, or else the stock wasn't thick enough. In any case, he was about fifty pounds shy.

Eddie, the trucker, was waiting for him. "Well?" he said, leaning forward against his hand truck.

"Wait a minute," Manny said. "It's too light. I got to check with Stiletti."

"Makes no difference to me," Eddie said, grinning. His wrinkled face was like a prune with a smile.

Manny wrote the time down on his time sheet. He looked for

Stiletti in the spread room, but the supervisor wasn't there; and he wasn't in the next room, either.

Manny passed the union steward. "Looking for Stiletti," he explained.

"When you want 'em, you can't find 'em, and when you don't want 'em, they're all over you," the steward, Frankie, said.

Manny nodded, then crossed the department, passed a storage area and approached the main office.

Stiletti was sitting inside, reading the paper, a cup of coffee at his side.

"Hey!" Manny shouted. Stiletti looked up. "The weight on that last roll's not right. Too light. You want me to run another coat or let it go?"

"Just a minute. I'll take a look." The supervisor stood up and, leaving his coffee by the desk, hurried across the room. "Come on," he said. Manny followed.

Stiletti was a short, flat-footed man in his early fifties. He waddled as he walked, knees slack and toes turned out, arms hanging limply by his sides. He wore checkered brown slacks and a light tan shirt, with neatly polished wing-tip brown shoes. "Hurry up!"

Stiletti's face was flat. His large tinted glasses seemed pasted on, and his jaws were constantly moving, as if he was chewing a cud.

They reached Manny's machine. The finished roll still hung on the scale.

Stiletti squinted, looking at the weight. "Goddamn," he breathed. "All right. Run another coat."

Manny reached for the pulley. "Okay," he said. "I guess the stock they made up first shift was too light."

"Just run another coat," Stiletti snapped, turning to go.

"Okay. By the way," he called after him. "I put six minutes down on the sheet, to cover the time I lost."

"What?"

"Yeah. I had to go find you and ask about the weight. It took about six minutes."

"Six minutes! It took thirty seconds!" Stiletti raised both arms. "Come on, Manny!"

"No, it *didn't*. I couldn't find you. I walked all around. Ask Frankie."

"That's part of your job," Stiletti said. "You don't get any down time for that."

"Bull *shit!*" Manny said. "I was trying to find you. Ask Frankie. I could have put another roll on and run it, but I didn't. I took the time out to stop the machine, go find you, and ask. Like Stu said."

"It's all the same. All part of your job."

"And what about all the talk about quality?"

"I'm not signing for it," Stiletti said, shaking his head. He turned to go, jaws working away.

"I'm not going to get screwed out of six minutes!" Manny shouted. Eddie was watching from the end of the room. So were Sal and Hernando, the other spreaders. "I mean, it isn't even worth *arguing* about. Just six minutes!"

Stiletti turned quickly towards him. "I've had enough of you chiseling time," he said. "Yesterday it was two minutes on a roll change. The other day it was five minutes extra cleaning up. Every day it's something else!"

"Every day there's problems on this machine!"

"My ass! If there's problems, it's your job to fix them. That's what you get paid for."

"I don't get paid to look for you! That's legitimate down time!"

"You want to look at the job standards? You can see for yourself."

"I do a damn good job. You know that. A lot of times I don't even put down when I lose two minutes here, five there. But. . . ."

"I don't care! If you don't want to work by the standards, you can go home!"

"Goddamn it!" Manny shouted. "There ain't no time in the standards for looking for a supervisor who isn't there!"

"I was right there, Manny. In the office."

"How was I supposed to know that?"

"Look. I'm not arguing any more. You're not going to chisel me out of any more time."

Manny threw his putty knife on the floor. "I'm not chiseling you out of anything. All I want is six minutes of down time I got coming to me."

Stiletti backed away again. "We've been over this already. Stu Grandy said. . . ."

"It's not coming out of *your* pocket!" Manny cried. "Why the hell are you so worried about it?"

Stiletti looked up. "Because I'm sick and tired of your attitude, Manny. It's got to stop. Believe me. I've gone out of my way to help you. I've even helped you clean up when you got in a mess. . . ."

"I never asked you to help!"

"But I have."

"So you want me to be grateful? What you mean is, you want me to lose the six minutes. Six minutes is fifty-five cents." He turned his pocket inside out. "That's what you're always doing. A quarter here. Fifty cents there. Taking it right out of my pocket." He jumped up and down.

"Don't yell at me!" Stiletti said.

"Bull shit!"

"I'm not signing it." He started out of the room.

Manny threw his gloves down on the floor. "I'm going to the union," he called loudly. "Enough is enough. And you can sign for that time, too."

He marched angrily into the adjoining room. Frankie, a rangy kid about twenty-five with a tousled head of red hair looked up at him. "Yeah?"

"Stiletti won't sign for six minutes of down time," Manny explained. "You saw me looking for him. I couldn't find him, and now he wants me to pay for the time myself."

"He won't sign the sheet?"

"No. I mean, it may seem small to you. But it's fifty-five cents to me. On top of everything else they take."

"Right. Okay. Tell me all the details."

Manny explained. Stiletti walked up to the other side of the calendar, jaws working, shaking his head. "The policy's already been set, Frankie. That time's in the standard."

"No, it's not!" Manny said. "*You're* the one trying to chisel me." He pointed at the clock. "I get the six minutes plus all this time, too."

Stiletti winked knowingly at Frankie, as if to joke about Manny.

"I don't know, Lou," Frankie said.

"Go ask Stu Grandy," Manny said. "We just had a meeting with him. He said to shut down if we had any questions, go ask the supervisor. They're so worried about quality. . . ."

Stiletti kept shaking his head, smiling as if Manny was some kind of lunatic.

"You ask Stu," Manny repeated. "I'll be back at my machine." He went back to the spread room, furious. They were always trying to screw you out of everything they could!

He started running the next coat, mulling over the arguments while he poured stock onto the fabric.

In ten minutes, Frankie came by. "He says, if you need the time at the end of the night, he'll sign for it, then."

"That's no good," Manny said. "I deserve that time, and I want it now."

"But will you be short?"

"I been short every night this week!" he said. He paused. "Did you ask Stu?"

"Not yet."

"Ask him. Stiletti's angry 'cause I caught him drinking coffee and reading the paper."

"Okay."

Manny went back to his machine. He worked rapidly, splattering the stock about. Now he was behind. He had to make up the time. The machine whirred along.

Frankie returned. "It's okay," he said. "You were right. Stu said that's the way it's supposed to be."

"All right!" he grinned at the steward. "I knew it! Thanks."

"It's okay. That Stiletti's a real son of a bitch."

"He's an asshole," Manny said. "They told the supervisors some of 'em were going to go, and he's trying to be a worse bastard than all the others and impress the front office."

"Yeah. Well, okay then." Frankie left.

A few minutes later Stiletti appeared. Hands on his hips, knees bowed out, he watched Manny work. Then, without saying a word, he walked away and returned with a tachymeter which he held against the spinning rubber roll. "Going pretty fast, aren't you?"

"I don't know." Manny needed the extra speed to get his percentage. All the spreaders sped the machines up to 50 or 55. If they didn't, they couldn't get their quota.

"Turn it down, Manny."

"What!"

"You're going fifty-three. Turn it down," Stiletti snapped. "Or do you want to get written up."

Manny lurched forward and turned the machine down, then spun around at Stiletti. "So just because I ask for a lousy six minutes, you're going to get back at me and turn the machine down."

"You're going too fast."

"Now you're taking five bucks right out of my pocket. Just because I asked for what I had coming to me."

"Don't shout at me."

"What do you expect me to do! Everybody runs at fifty-three and you know it."

"The standard is forty-two. Sometimes I let you go forty-six."

"Thanks a lot."

"Manny, you were going too fast."

"And of course your turning the machine down's got nothing to do with me arguing over down time."

Stiletti shook his head and turned, without answering, and began walking away.

"Son of a bitch!" Manny called.

Eddie came over. "He's a real one, ain't he?"

"Turned the speed down because I was right. Like some little baby, trying to get back at me."

"I know."

"They hang it over you all the time. Be a good boy, and they'll let you speed it up so you can make your money. Then, whenever they want to get you, they just slow you down."

"The standards don't make sense to begin with."

"You can't make your money the way it's set up."

"I know it."

"He's scared because they're going to get rid of some supervisors. I hope they fire his ass!"

Eddie shook his head. "Why do you think people are always bidding out of this department. No one wants to work for him."

"*I* sure don't."

"He don't know how to deal with you like a person."

"Tells me not to yell at him. After all this."

"Hey, was you going to hit him?"

"Naw."

"I thought you might. Wally, he says he never saw Stiletti so worried. When you threw the putty knife."

"I was pissed."

"Wally says, if you're gonna hit him, let him know so he can come watch." Eddie grinned, then started coughing.

Manny tried to smile back. "I don't want to hit anybody. I just want to make my bucks like anyone else."

"They don't make it easy for you."

"No. They make you fight 'em for every penny."

"I know."

"So I got my six minutes and the ten minutes spent talking with Frankie. And he sticks me for five bucks. Which is what I lose when I'm slowed down."

"Yep. He's trying to teach you a lesson."

"I guess so."

The rest of the night, Stiletti didn't show his face in the spread room. But, as they were all getting ready to go home, he approached a group of workers.

"Hey, Stanley," he said, smiling broadly, "Give the ol' lady one for me tonight, huh." He made an obscene gesture with his arm and laughed, encouraging the other workers to join in.

Several grinned. It was an old joke.

"Yeah. You try and get it up tonight, Stanley."

"Else ol' Stiletti, he take your place."

"Stanley, he's no good no more."

More people laughed. Stiletti was grinning now, his jaws grinding away, his body bent forward.

"I'm not laughing at this guy's jokes," Manny said. "He just took five bucks out of my pocket tonight. He's no friend of mine."

Stiletti froze. The other workers turned towards Manny.

"What do you mean?"

"Just 'cause I made him give me six minutes down time, he comes and turns my machine down. That cost me five bucks. That's money to put food on my table, you know. Now he wants to play buddy-buddy."

A few workers moved away from Stiletti.

"Oh yeah?"

"Uh-huh. It don't come out of *his* pocket. Hell, he's even costing the *company* money, slowing me down like that. Some supervisor! I come here to work, and he wants to play games."

A few more workers, clearing their throats and putting their coats on, turned away from Stiletti.

"Take it easy, Manny," Harris, one of the pro-company workers called.

Manny ignored him. Stiletti was now left with a handful of pro-company workers and stoolies.

"'Hey," Eddie whispered to the others, loudly. "You shoulda seen Stiletti's face when Manny threw his putty knife down on the floor. Oh, Jesus! I thought Manny was going to hit him. Stiletti turned all white and started backing out of the room." He laughed so hard he had to wipe his eyes.

The others laughed, too. "Some day, he will get beat up," Hernando said. "Always leaning on people. They'll find him face-down in the parking lot one night."

"Serve him right."

"He thinks he's better than us. Wait till they lay *him* off. Then he'll cry to join the union like Mario did."

"No way!"

It was quitting time.

"Well, let's go. Manny, Ed."

The workers, neat in their clean clothes, moved out.

"Hey, Andy. You down for a beer?"

"Always!"

"Manny?"

"Why not?"

"Got to relax, my man."

"Take a load off your mind."

"Let's all drop by Sam's."

Manny smiled. "Hey, you guys are all right." He felt better.

Moving

Andy hadn't wanted to move. All his friends were in the old neighborhood. But Ma said they had to, 'cause she wasn't going to be beat up again by that crazy Warren who'd already attacked her twice.

The week before, he'd broken the door down to get at her. He was out of his mind, strung out on drugs or something. And he'd got it in his mind that Ma was "his woman," just 'cause she'd been nice to him once or twice. And then, 'cause she wouldn't go along with it, he'd tried to teach her a lesson.

So Ma said they all had to move, and no one could know about it. Donna helped them find a place. And one night after dark they moved everything they had as quick as they could, with Donna and her husband and another friend to help, and left their old apartment empty, with the doors open and the keys in the locks, and the floors littered with garbage and broken toys.

They left no forwarding address and didn't tell anyone where they had gone.

Andy begged to go back "just once" and explain to his friends where he had gone and why. But Ma said no. She didn't want anyone knowing, or else Warren would be breaking down their door again.

The day after they moved, she took him and Crissie and Sharon and registered them in the school down the street.

"But how'm I going to make all new friends?" he cried. "You can't just come into class in the middle of the year.... It's hard!"

"I know it's hard," Ma said, "and I'm sorry you got to do it. But that's the way it's got to be. So we might as well try and make the best of it."

"All right," he said, unhappily. "I'll try. But it won't do any good. I know...."

"Just try."

"I will."

It wasn't a question of his trying. He always tried hard at what he was supposed to do. He was afraid of failing. Deep in the back of his mind was a grinning monster with a pock-marked face who kept saying over and over again he'd never amount to a hill of beans, and that's what bothered him.

The new neighborhood was tougher than the old one. The kids were all different types—Black kids and Spanish kids, and Irish kids, and kids with Italian names and kids with American names, and kids with weird African names like Nbulu and Nkomo that sounded like coconuts knocking against one another.

The Spanish were always fighting the other kids, and the Blacks got angry if you said the wrong thing. Sometimes a couple of them would push against you for no reason and threaten to "cut your dick off." And the white kids were always picking on each other, too.

There was lots of name-calling in the street and in the school.

And lots of fighting. Especially on Friday afternoon and Saturdays.

As far as he could tell, most of the kids came from the same kind of homes he did. There wasn't much money for new clothes and shoes, and kids wore hand-me-downs from older brothers and sisters, or cousins. Nobody had much money to spend at the store, and the little kids were always holding their dimes and quarters tight in their fists, afraid someone was going to take it away from them.

Some of the other kids' mothers were on welfare like Ma. A lot of families were messed up. A lot of fathers drank. It was like Cambridge, but worse.

School was a joke. During lunch, the kids threw food around the cafeteria, flipping peas with their spoons and trying to stick gobs of vanilla pudding or creamed spinach on the ceiling.

There was a lot of noise, with some kids grabbing other kids' lunch and racing around. The aides wouldn't stop them, 'cause the tougher kids said they'd beat them up if they tried, and anyhow they were just old ladies with arthritis and swollen feet.

During class, some of the older kids would stand up when the teacher turned her back and make loud sucky noises or squeeze farting sounds against their armpits. Then the teacher would spin around and get mad, and the whole class would be in trouble, and no one would be able to have any recess because the class had been "bad."

Sometimes, the principal would come in, shaking his fat sweaty head, and tell them that none of them was going anywhere without education, and here they were, wasting the one chance they had, and if they didn't straighten up and "clean up their act," then they'd wind up in jail, or working in stinky factories like their Ma or Pa, or being on welfare with a bunch of ungrateful kids like themselves.

That talk bothered Andy. He didn't want to wind up in jail. He didn't want to wind up without a job. And he didn't want to get stabbed to death in the street, or killed in some race riot.

It was hard for him to concentrate. Thoughts would suddenly rise up in his mind, like dinosaurs coming out of some swamp, and he'd forget what he was doing. Or else his thoughts would get thin, like all the water was going out of them, and they'd start floating away and he couldn't grab them back.

He worried about being dumb.

He's never made good grades, and now he was in the worst part of the class because of mistakes he made the first few weeks. The school had different rules than he'd learned before. Like, writing his name on the left side of the page instead of on the right side. Or putting the name of the school underneath his own name instead of next to it. Or underlining all the titles of his themes.

Because he did things the way he'd been taught in his old school at first, the teacher yelled at him and made him feel stupid. And, seeing the teacher yell at him, the other kids felt they could tease him, and they did.

It didn't help to talk to Ma about it.

"Look," she'd say. "You just try. Sit there with the book in front of you and *con*centrate."

"I *do*!" he shouted. "I *do* try. It don't do any good!"

"I don't want you ending up like me," she'd say. "I never learned to read, all through the tenth grade. They kept promoting me, but they didn't do me any favors. Now look at me. I can't get a job, and I got to stare at the paper for half an hour just to read one lousy story."

He hated it when she started on that.

"An' you're just like I was," she'd go on. "You started out seeing your b's and d's backwards. You didn't know whether to write with your left or your right hand...." She'd shake her head, then smooth her stringy sand-colored hair back with her skinny fingers. "An' God knows, you don't get nothing from your Pa!"

Then she'd lean forward and grip him with those starey blue eyes: "If it takes a little more time, you go ahead. You ain't *smart* like Chrissie. And you ain't got the spunk *Sharon* has. So you got to work five times harder for anything you get."

It was like living under a curse. She had this problem. Now he had it, too. It was in his blood, he couldn't get away from it. And the teacher didn't care if he learned anything at all.

His teacher wrote home saying he had a spelling problem, a

reading problem and a conduct problem.

He threw the note away and told the teacher Ma had seen it. She didn't even call to check up on him.

What worried him most was getting along with the other kids.

In the beginning, no one had wanted to play with him. Every kid already had a best friend, and there wasn't any room for him to break in.

When the teacher came down on him, the kids started teasing: "Dumbo," they'd call him. And "dunce-head."

They'd gang up on him. Two guys would come up behind him, one on either side, and bump him with their hips. Or try and knock his books out of his arms. Or take his hat. Or knock him down the stairs.

Once he punched a kid hard in the ribs, and the kid left him alone. But it didn't make a friend.

Two kids who jostled him a lot were called Steve and Poke. Steve was slender like himself, but Poke was fat, with little pig-eyes staring out of a smooth pink face.

One day when they'd tripped him up for the two-thousandth time, he turned on them:

"All right!" he shouted. "I'm *sick* of you guys teasing me all the time. You think it's *easy* to come into a new school and try and make friends, well you're wrong! So you can just stop *bugging* me or there's going to be trouble!"

"Trouble," Poke said, imitating him. "There's going to be trouble!"

"All right! Stop laughing!" He clenched his fists. "All right! You asked for it!"

He threw himself at Poke, swinging wildly.

Poke, who outweighed him by about twenty pounds, grabbed him around the waist and squeezed. Then he threw him on the ground and fell on top of him.

"Goddamnit!" Andy yelled, kicking and clawing. "Get off me!"

Poke squirmed to stay on top of him, punching his stomach.

" 'Atta boy, Poke," Steve shouted. "Give it to him!"

"You fat... blubber!" Andy yelled, unable to move the heavier kid off his chest.

Poke ground his stumpy fingers in his ribs. "Give up? Give up?"

"No!"

He ground his fingers in his ribs again.

"All right. Yes. All right!" Andy shouted. "Just get offa me!"

Poke got off. His face was sweaty and bright red. "You're a tough little fucker, aren't you?" he said, breathing heavily.

"I just don't like being bugged all the time."

"Okay." Poke stood with his hands on his hips. "So the guy don't like being bugged." Then he grinned and held out his hand. "No hard feelings, then."

Andy looked at him, puzzled, then shook hands. "Okay."

"Well. I guess that means you're okay, then," Steve said.

That was how Andy made his first two friends.

Steve and Poke were both white. They told Andy they hated "niggers" and they hated "spics." If they had to, they'd get along with them in school, but they hated them all the same.

"Some of 'em can't even speak English," Steve said. "What the hell good are they?"

"Like, what do they want here?" Poke said. "That's what my Dad says."

"The spics come here to get on welfare. Right? An' then they bring their whole family."

"That's why we got to stick with our own."

"Is it?" Andy asked.

"Sure. You think about it. You'll see."

Andy didn't like the way they always made fun of Black and Spanish kids, but he went along with it because Poke and Steve were his only friends.

He wasn't even sure why he didn't like it. It just didn't seem that funny to him. Maybe it was 'cause he'd just gone through a lot of teasing himself, and he didn't think any kid should have to be treated that way.

One night he asked Tom, the man who'd started coming by the house to see Ma, what he thought about it.

"See, they make all these jokes. And try and get everyone to laugh. Only I don't think it's funny. But I don't know what to do."

Tom was a big burly guy with round shoulders and a tired face. "Just keep your mouth shut," he said.

"Why?"

" 'Cause you just got here. That's why. If you want to fit in, then you got to fit in with what the other kids do. If you want to be different, then you'll be different all by yourself."

"But it ain't right, is it?"

"Kid, I don't know what's right and what ain't anymore." He took a deep breath. "There's been a lot of trouble between white and Black here, and with the Spanish. You know? You got to understand these things."

Tom was leaning so close to him, Andy could smell the beer on his breath.

"You know what I mean?" the man said.

"I don't know." He stopped, feeling the man's eyes on his face. "I mean, yeah. Yeah, I understand."

"All right, then," Tom said, dismissing him. "Then you don't have to ask any more questions, do you? Anyway, what I hear is that you got enough to keep you busy, just doing your schoolwork. Ain't that right?"

He felt he was being put down. "Uh-huh," he answered.

The monster was laughing again. He realized it had been a mistake talking to Tom in the first place.

One day after school, he sat on the front steps and watched what was going on.

His sister Chrissie had already made friends with the girls on the street and was out with them. His other sister Sharon was nowhere in sight.

A bunch of kids his age were playing football in the street, three against three. One or two others were riding their bikes.

There wasn't much traffic at all.

The street was made up of three-decker houses without yards or driveways, jammed right up against one another. Almost every house had a front porch—some of them had porches on every floor—and a couple of steps going down to the sidewalk.

The roofs of the houses were absolutely flat.

Down one end of the street, to the right, was a small grocery store, where everyone went for bread and milk, cigarettes and ice cream. Down the other direction, to the left and around the corner, were some more stores—a drugstore, laundromat, and a meat market—and a bar across the street.

The kids on his street were white. Two blocks over, the Blacks began. And the Spanish were somewhere nearby, but he wasn't sure where.

It was getting on into November. Somewhere, someone was burning a pile of leaves, and the smell filled the air. It reminded him of the time they had visited his Grandpa and Grandma in New Hampshire. That was a long time ago, a couple years after his Pa had left, and Ma had taken him and the girls to visit Pa's family and ask for some money.

Grandpa still lived on a farm, a place smelling of apples and burning leaves.

That was the only time he'd seen his grandparents. They hadn't given Ma any money, so she never went back. They never wrote to keep in touch. They didn't send presents at Christmas or cards on the kids' birthdays. It was like they didn't care.

It was getting cold. On days like this, the sky had a way of turning icy-blue, without a cloud in it to spoil the color. He could see it over the flat tops of the houses, the dome of the sky arching high overhead. When it got dark, it was like someone dimming the lights, bit by bit, ever so slowly, so that at first you didn't even notice it, 'cause your eyes were adjusted to it, and then you'd suddenly realize you couldn't see down the other end of the street, or you'd try and catch a football and find out you couldn't follow it through the air anymore, and it'd be like a fine gray cloud drifting down over the whole city, heavier and heavier, until you had to squint just to see a house away. And then the street lights would go on, and the kids' mothers would be calling them to come in for dinner, and the streets would empty out, except for the older kids leaning against the sides of the buildings, smoking cigarettes, and the men coming home from work.

He asked Ma about it one day:

"Where do all these Spanish kids come from, and why do they come here?"

She looked up. "I dunno. Same as anyone else, I guess."

"But why don't they stay in their own country?"

"Maybe it's better here."

"The kids say they all want to go on welfare."

She sounded her hard, dry laugh, more like a cough than a laugh. "Andy, I never knew anybody crazy enough to want to go on welfare. Not even if they was Puerto Ricans."

"The kids say the same thing about Black people."

"Don't seem that way to me."

"So why do they come?"

"Andy, I don't know. You got to ask them, not me. Maybe they ain't got nothing where they are, so what we got looks like a lot. Then they come here, and see it ain't so much after all. I dunno. Once they're here, they got to make the best of it."

"Yeah," Andy said, thinking it over. "That makes sense."

Ma sighed. "Don't seem to me we got so much we got to worry about someone else getting it, too. Or begrudge somebody the couple bucks they get from welfare."

"But the kids all call each other names, and there's an awful lot of fighting and all," he blurted out.

"Well...." Ma was quiet. "You just got to deal with that, too."

"Uh-huh."

"You got to figure out what you think is right."

He nodded.

"One thing you got to remember. If you're hungry, then you got to eat. If you're sleepy, then you got to sleep. No matter who you are. There's a whole lot that's the same about people." She paused, lighting a cigarette and tossing the match in the round glass ashtray on the kitchen table. "I guess there's a lot of

100

differences, too. But they never hit me as the most important part." She inhaled.

"Ma, don't *smoke*!" he whined. "It ain't good for you!"

"Don't tell your mother what to do!"

The next day Andy studied himself in the mirror. He was scrawny, no doubt about that. Sharon was slender like Ma. Chrissie was supposed to look like their Pa. But no one could say who *he* took after.

He had a tense mouth and a sharp, upturned nose. His hair was sandy-brown. His eyes were hazel. He noticed some freckles on his nose, nobody in the family had freckles. And his ears stuck out.

He saw a few pimples.

"Startin' to be a teenager," Tom had teased. "Only eleven, and he's already starting out on his acne."

"Shut up," he said to himself in the mirror. He didn't like the things Tom said to him.

He pursed his lips, then made a scary face; then combed his hair over his eyes, trying to look cool.

It didn't work.

He tried combing it off to one side....

"Andy!" Ma called. "What you doing in there?"

"Nothin'."

"Then come on out."

He came out. Ma was in the kitchen heating water for tea, wearing a blue blouse and jeans and smoking again. He didn't say anything.

"You want something to eat?"

He shook his head. "Naw. Thanks."

The kettle rumbled, then hesitantly began whistling. Ma turned the flame off before the whistle became shrill and steady and poured some steaming water into her cup, then plopped in a tea bag and put the kettle back on the stove.

"So how's school going, Andy?"

"Aw. Okay."

"You learning anything?"

"I guess."

She nodded. "Listen, I might be getting a job. Maybe next week."

"Going off welfare?"

"Well...not yet. But if this works out, maybe I could."

"Uh-huh."

"Anyway, I want you to start keeping an eye on Sharon. You got to be the man of the family. Chrissie can take care of herself. She's pretty mature. But I'm worried about Sharon. I don't know what she'll get into next."

Sharon had already been getting into trouble, but he didn't want to tattle. She was twelve, a year older than him. And Chrissie was thirteen.

Sharon had been telling Ma she was going to school every day, but in fact she was playing hookey and hanging out with kids down on Dewsnapp Street, smoking cigarettes and who knew what else.

Sharon was always getting into trouble. Last year, she'd been stealing from Kresge's. And the year before, there was a whole thing about her taking rides with strange men and almost getting into real bad trouble.

"Okay. I'll keep an eye on her," he said.

"Good." Ma sat down at the kitchen table.

"Ma, you look tired,"

"I am."

He leaned forward. "What's with Tom?"

She didn't look up. "Nothing."

"Is he going to be our new dad?"

"Jesus, Andy!" she cried, sitting up and waving her hands at him. "I don't know. How the hell would I know a thing like that? I just barely met the man."

"But he spends a lot of time here."

"So?"

"So nothing." He shrugged and stuck his hands in his pockets and looked at the floor. "I just wondered."

"Do you want him to be your dad?" she said after a while.

He hesitated. "Naw...not really."

She jabbed the cigarette out in the ashtray. "Well, we'll just have to see...."

The kitchen was quiet, except for the refrigerator humming. He knew he had homework to do, but he didn't want to.

"Ma...."

"What?"

"Do I look like my Pa?"

She examined him with an odd expression on her face. "Like your Pa?" For a minute she looked sad, like her mind had floated away. "I dunno. I guess, in some ways, you do."

"What ways?"

"Jesus, Andy! What do you want? I dunno. Maybe your eyes. The way you walk, a little."

"Uh-huh."

"Why?"

"No reason. I just wondered." He paused. "I mean, do I *act* like Pa?"

"How do you mean?"

He waved his hand. "I don't know. I mean, after all, I don't even *remember* him. I don't know what he was like...or anything."

"Mmm." She was quiet for a few minutes.

The refrigerator motor clicked off. There were shouts from the kids outside.

"I don't know," she said, abruptly standing up and bringing her empty cup to the sink. "I don't want to talk about it."

She was getting angry.

He felt he should stop, but he couldn't. "How come he don't ever write or call?"

"I don't know *that, either,*" she cried. "Some day when you find him, you can ask him!"

"Don't get mad."

"What am I supposed to do? When you sit asking me a bunch of dumb questions...."

The words stung. "That's right. Whatever I say is dumb. Whatever I do. Thanks a lot." He spun around and headed for the door.

"Andy, I didn't . . . ."

"Forget it," he shouted. "Sorry if I *bothered* you." He pulled the front door open, went out and slammed it after himself.

He felt bad as soon as he'd done it, but he was angry. How was he supposed to figure out what to do if everybody either put him down or didn't care, or wouldn't answer what he asked, or . . . . What the hell!

Kicking every stone or can that stood in his way, Andy headed for the playground, where most of the kids his age hung out.

It was a gray day, a fine mist was starting to come down, making everything damp. He could smell the ocean.

He'd forgotten to wear his jacket.

It was chilly, but he didn't care. He had on his flannel shirt, and a T-shirt under that. And besides, he didn't care.

When he reached the park, none of his new friends were around. Some older kids were smoking pot by the benches, and a few Black kids were playing basketball. Other than that, the park was empty.

He sat on a concrete ledge and put his head in his hands. "What a life," he said, half-aloud.

A bunch of Spanish kids came up the sidewalk towards him, then veered off to the side where there was a grassy area. One of them was carrying a soccer ball.

When they got to the area, they started kicking the ball back and forth, laughing, and chattering to one another in Spanish.

Andy watched them.

The sky was a dark, dingy color, the color of city streets. A breeze stirred up from the east. Now it was beginning to rain. Parts of the playground already had puddles from rain that morning, and the grassy area was muddied up.

One of the kids kicked the ball over towards Andy, and he bent over to get it and throw it back.

"Hey," one of them said all of a sudden. "You want to play?"

"What?"

"Yeah. You. You want to play?"

One of the others said something in Spanish, and a couple of the kids laughed. Andy didn't have to understand Spanish to know they'd said something about him. Probably that he didn't know how to play. Or that he was too skinny. Or maybe just that he was white.

A flash of fear went over him, and he wondered if they were going to beat him up or something. "Aw, what the hell," he said to himself. "The way this day has gone, I don't care if they do . . . ."

The kid who'd spoken to him came over closer and asked him again.

"Hey, thanks. But no thanks," he said, feeling stupid. "I don't know how to play. Football, maybe. But not soccer."

"But it's easy. And, anyway, we got an odd number, and you'd make the sides even."

"Yeah? Well, okay then." He slid off the ledge and joined them.

"See. This is all you do," the other said. "Kick it with your feet. Your hands can't touch the ball. But you can use your head, if you want. See?" He bounced the ball high in the air, off his head.

"Pisser!" Andy said, admiring the feat. He wondered how the kid could do that without it hurting.

"You all set?" the kid asked.

"Sure. Why not?"

"Okay. You're on our team, then. Let's go."

They started playing.

Once he got into it, Andy found it wasn't so hard, and soon he was running and sliding and kicking with the rest of them.

The kid's name was Carlos, and he was from Puerto Rico. One of the other kids, from Colombia, somewhere in South America, was as dark as any American Black man.

They played until it got so dark they couldn't see. Then they stopped. They were completely soaked.

"See ya later," the kids said to him.

"Yeah. See ya later. See ya, Carlos."

It struck him that this was the first time since he'd moved that anyone had just asked him into their group.

When he got home, dinner was on the table.

"Where you been?" Ma said.

"Playing ball."

"Well...." It looked like she was going to say something, but she didn't. "Just sit down and eat your dinner. Wash your hands first."

"Okay."

He hadn't been eating more than two minutes when the phone rang. It was Sharon's teacher.

Suddenly, Ma was yelling at the top of her voice. "What? Not for two weeks! Yes, I will. Yes, you bet! Thank you very much for calling."

She hung the phone up and stalked to the table.

"What is it?" Sharon asked, squirming in her chair.

"You know *damn* well what it is," Ma said. "You ain't been going to school for at least two weeks. Maybe more. What *have* you been doing? That's what *I'd* like to know." She grabbed Sharon by the back of the neck.

"Nothing!" Sharon screamed. "Nothing! Just smoking a couple cigarettes with the other girls."

"I don't *want* you smoking in the street!"

"All right. All right. I'll stop!"

"And what *else*?"

"Nothing! I swear. You can ask Angie."

"I ain't asking *any*body!" she dragged the girl into the bathroom and started hitting her with both hands. "Now that's enough!" she shouted.

Chrissie ran to the bathroom door. "Ma," she pleaded. "Please stop."

"God damn lying...." Ma cried. "That is one thing I will not take!" She grabbed a hairbrush and began hitting Sharon with the flat end.

"Ma!" Sharon cried. "Ow! Ma! Stop!"

Ma was beside herself. "I'll stop when I'm good and ready!"

"Ma!" Chrissie said again. "Please. Please stop. She'll be good."

"Go ahead and kill me!" Sharon cried suddenly. "You don't care anyway. Move here! Move there! Get yourself *this* boyfriend. Get yourself *that* boyfriend. What do you care about *us*?"

"Whatever I do, don't mean you can lie to me! I *never* lied to my own mother!

"You go to school," Ma screamed. "You hear! Every day. I don't want you pregnant at fourteen, going on welfare. Okay? That goes for all of you." She shook Sharon by the shoulders. "You understand?"

The door opened, and Tom stepped in. Ma didn't see him.

"Okay," Sharon said. "Okay. Okay. Okay."

"I'm disgusted with the whole lot of you," Ma said, turning towards the kitchen again.

"*All* of us? What did *I* do?" Chrissie wailed. "Jesus Christ! I didn't do nothing!"

"All right. So you didn't do nothing. But the bunch of you is driving me crazy. I mean it."

"What's going on?" Tom said.

"Nothing," Chrissie said.

"I just found out Sharon hasn't been going to school for two weeks," Ma said, holding her hands out to him, as if for help.

"So? What's the big fuss?" Tom took a step towards the table. He was staggering, off-balance.

"You've been drinking!"

"I'm hungry."

She rushed up to him, as if she was on fire. "No! Get out. Get out, Tom. Right now!" She pushed on his chest and arms, trying to turn him around and face him out the door. "I don't want you in here now. Get out!"

"I ain't even moved in, and you're throwing me out?"

"I don't want to talk about it. Just go, Tom. Please go!"

The children had all gathered behind her, standing between her and the table.

"Christ, what'd I say?"

She pushed him towards the door. "Just go."

"I'm going. I'm going." He stumbled the few feet towards the door, then braced himself against the doorjamb and turned around. "But I'm not going to forget this. You had one man and lost him. Then you had another and lost him. Now I'm starting to understand why . . . ." Then, as if he thought she was going to throw something at him, he turned again, one arm raised, and began down the stairs, leaning against the wall for suport, stumbling down.

Ma slammed the door shut and ran into the room, her face in her hands.

The following afternoon, Andy went back to the park. Steve and Poke came with him. It was a dismal, chilly day, with gray clouds low in the sky, looking like it was going to rain some more.

They hung around the benches for a while, talking about school.

After a few minutes, Andy spotted Carlos entering the park from the other end.

Poke saw him, too. "Hey! More fuckin' spics in this park . . . ."

Steve looked up. "You're right."

"Look," Andy said. "Do we have to talk like that?"

"Why not?" Poke said. "Don't hurt anyone."

Seeing Andy, Carlos moved hesitantly towards them.

"Hi there," Andy said, waving.

"You know him?"

"Uh-huh."

"How come?"

"Just 'cause."

Carlos reached them. Andy shook his hand. "How ya

doing?"

"Okay." He hung back, hands in his pockets.

"These are my buddies, Poke and Steve."

"Hiya."

Poke didn't hold out his hand. "Hiya," he said, his voice flat.

A cold breeze gusted past them. For a few seconds, no one spoke.

Andy felt his features tighten up. Why didn't anybody say anything!

"Yeah. Well...." Carlos said, taking a step backwards like he was going to leave.

"Hey...." Andy said, his mouth suddenly dry.

"See ya later."

"Hey," Poke said, taking a step forward. "Does your Pa have a job? Or is your whole family on welfare?"

Andy stared at him.

"What's *that* supposed to mean?" Carlos asked.

"What do you think?"

"Hey," Andy said, moving to take hold of Poke's arm. "Wait a minute . . . ."

Poke shook himself free. "Wait a minute yourself. I want an answer." He paused looking at Carlos.

It was suddenly very tense.

"You want an answer?"

Poke nodded slowly. "Uh-huh."

"Okay. Shove it up your ass! That's my answer."

"Hey! Nobody talks to my buddy like that," Steve said, pushing Carlos back with the flat of his hand.

"Then he shouldn't talk to me like that!"

"Take it back!" Poke shouted.

"Fuck you!"

"Hey!" Andy shouted. "Hold it!"

Poke swung at Carlos but missed. Steve jumped forward, grabbing him by the chest, pinning his arms behind him.

"Okay, Poke," he cried. "I got him. Teach him a lesson. Pop him one in the stomach."

Poke shoved a fist in Carlos' stomach.

"All right! All right!" Andy yelled, throwing himself at the three of them. "You guys cut it out!"

Poke shoved a shoulder in his face. "You stay out of this."

"Cut it out!"

Carlos twisted around and kicked Steve in the shin, just as Andy was pulling him back.

"Ow! Son of a bitch!"

"Come on! Break it up!"

"He kicked me!"

"Forget it!"

"I won't." Steve grabbed Carlos again and pushed him to the ground.

"Leave him alone!"

Poke turned on him. "Hey, what's *with* you, anyway? What do you care what happens to him?"

"I'm sick of all these fights and name-calling, that's all. It makes me want to throw up!"

"It does?" Poke turned to Steve, who still had Carlos down. "You know what I think? I think Andy has a streak of spic in him. That's what."

Steve looked up. "You know? You just might be right. Is that right, Andy? You got a little spic blood in you?"

Something inside him gave way. "You guessed it!" Andy cried, hurtling through the air against Steve and knocking him over. "That's right! You guessed it!" He was kicking and clawing to pull Steve off Carlos, ramming his shoulder into Poke's side. "I'm a spic, too. Him and me, we're both spics. Ain't we, Carlos? That's right. I'm a spic, too. A fuckin' spic."

Poke hit him in the back of the head, and he winced. For an instant he was dizzy; then it passed. He swung back, connected, took a punch in the mouth, swung back again.

"You want to hit *him,* you got to beat *me* up, too!"

With each punch, the monster was taking a beating.

Don

The plant was a sweatshop, an old L-shaped wooden building three stories high. Its red paint was cracked and peeling, and its windows were black with dust. Inside, 300 workers made heels and soles out of synthetic rubber.

It was the largest factory in town. When the wind blew from the northeast, sulfur fumes swept through the streets, penetrating the tenements where many workers lived, overpowering the smell of onions, cabbage and frying meat. When the wind was still, the fumes rose to form a yellow haze high in the air, making the people below cough and rub their eyes.

Inside, the acrid odor clung to the workers' clothes. Different dusts and chemicals set them wheezing, and there were frequent fires. A millroom explosion the previous summer had hurt five people.

The Prep Department on the second floor was filled with a

fine haze of dust. Many workers wore paper bags on their heads to keep it out of their hair. A few wore masks over their mouths and noses.

The heart of this department was its three Banburies, giant churning machines which mixed batches of rubber stock. Fed by the other workers—the scalemen, rubber weighman and colorman—the Banbury operators worked nonstop: guiding their machines through their cycles, maintaining the right temperature, adding the different ingredients at the correct time, and, finally, releasing the steaming batches through the gates onto the massive roller mills on the floor below.

Metal cans clanked over the metal rails. Steam hissed from the pipes. There was the hum of the Banburies, the grinding noise of the rubber weighman's guillotine, the squealing of the scalemen's elevator as it ascended the rails. And amid the general clamor was the sound of the workers calling to one another, shouting, swearing and singing, yelling for the forklift truck, laughing, whistling up the chute for more supplies. The men's voices rose and fell like ships on a swelling sea.

The No. 2 Banbury operator was in his early twenties. He was six feet tall and husky, wearing a white T-shirt, bell bottoms and work boots. His face was beaded with sweat, and from time to time he wiped his forehead with his glove or tossed his tangled blond hair back away from his eyes with a jerk of the head. Usually he had a tired, bored expression on his face, but when the gate stuck or a can jammed his finger against the rail, he got angry and cried out, slamming the empty cans hard against the Banbury door.

This was Don. He'd been working at the plant just under a year.

The men ate lunch in the locker room at the far end of the floor, sitting along a narrow row of benches between the wall and the first row of lockers. Even after they washed up, they were smeared with dirt. Angel, the colorman, was usually bathed in whatever color stock they were running, scarlet red from head to foot, bright blue, or flaming yellow.

Most of them brought lunch. A few, like John from Trinidad,

brought rice with meat or vegetables, wrapped in tin foil, which they heated on the steam pipes and ate with metal forks and spoons which they kept in their lockers. Others went downstairs to buy food from the lunch truck: hot soup or chili in paper cups, submarine sandwiches, cakes, potato chips, soft drinks. Then they gathered on the bench, welcoming their twenty minutes to sit down, and talked about the latest plant rumor, what they'd done the night before, or the morning paper.

One cold February day, Don took his lunch out of his locker and sat down next to Vasco, who ran the No. 3 Banbury.

Vasco grinned up at him, "Working hard today?"

"You know it."

"Got to learn how to run Banbury. Take minute off here. Minute there. Get extra batches that way. More money." He was a light-skinned Black man from the Azores with a hoarse squeaky voice, an old hand in the department. His face was broad and earnest, with small twinkling eyes and a flat nose. Vasco was an efficient worker who knew how to cut corners and speed himself up for a few extra cents an hour. Trained in almost every job in the department, he often worked an extra half-shift, filling in where the company needed him.

"I know," Don said. "But the damned gate is sticking today."

"Damn gate *always* sticks. When they run shitty 702 stock. You got to watch it. Watch machine every minute. First time you turn your back, BOOM! It fuck you up."

Don unwrapped his sandwich and took a bite. "I know."

"If they keep running bad stock," Andy the smallscaleman said leaning over, "you just punch your card. Say you have to shut down and clean the machine." He waved his hand. "They got to go along with that."

"That's right," Vasco said. "And if they give you any trouble go to union."

"What good'll *that* do?" Frank said. He was rubber weighman for No. 1 Banbury. "When was the last time *you* saw the union take anything up?"

"What you want? You go *anyway*," Vasco said. "Make some noise." He nodded. "They back you up."

"Ahh, the union's as weak as a wet paper bag," Frank said.

"They won't take up the littlest grievance unless you light a fire under them."

"That's the way it's always been, so why don't you shut up," John from Trinidad, the dustman, said. "You want to complain, keep it to yourself." He sat down on the floor and unwrapped his lunch, steaming in its tin foil. "Everybody complain today."

The argument began drawing in other workers.

"The union's only what we make it," Andy said. "That's how I see it." He was a wiry Black man in his mid-forties wearing a hot dog vendor's white cap to keep the dust off his head. "Can't blame Johnny for everything."

"Naw. Johnny tries his best," Harry, the forklift driver said, waving his soup spoon in the air for emphasis.

"Johnny's sold out," the largescaleman, Stein, said. "Everybody knows that. But what're you going to do about it?"

"Good question," Frank said.

"Can't fight City Hall," Vic said in a sing-song voice. He was No. 2 Banbury's rubber weighman.

"So what do I do?" Don asked. "Shut it down or not?"

"You shut it down," Vasco said, impatiently. "That's that. Johnny back you up. Now eat your lunch."

The others nodded and shifted their positions on the bench. Frank popped open a can of tonic. Stein lit up a cigarette. For a moment, they ate in silence. A thin chill draft blew in through a crack in the window. It was cold outside. Flakes of snow flew about the edge of the roof like feathers. Smoke from the pressroom gushed into the air through tube-shaped stacks on the roof, tumbling about wildly, spinning, soaring above the plant where the wind attacked it, thinned it out and scattered it—still rising and whirling—into fine, almost invisible particles which would come down hundreds of yards away with the snow, falling on the town.

The silence was broken by a gravelly voice with an Appalachian accent: "Way-yull. Looks like thur takin' maysurements o' the machines downstay-yers." Pete, the Banbury operator of No. 1, entered the room. He was an older man with a pot belly, wearing baggy grey pants, a tattered blue T-shirt and a grey cap, stained with grease and carbon black.

"What's that mean?" Paul, the sweeper asked.

"Prub'ly goin' tuh build 'em in Missi'ppi. Ship some mo-wer work ott."

"So what do that say for us?"

"Hard tuh say," he said, sitting down.

"Don' say nuthin' good," Andy said. "You can bet your ass on that."

"Company mess with you just to mess with you."

"Oh. They got some idee. Prub'ly find ott soon."

"They'll send more work down South, make more money," Frank said. "They ain't got a union down there. Cheaper wages. You wait and see."

"Profit," Vic sang. "It's the name of the game."

"They ain't dumb."

"They got you coming and going."

"It's the name of the game," Vic sang again, reaching under the bench for his morning paper. "The name of the game."

Paul leaned forward, rubbing his hands together. He was a nervous Black youth with fast darting eyes and long thin fingers. "Hey," he said, his voice uncertain. "I need this job, you know...."

"Oh, I wooden worry about it now," Pete said. "Thur's always rumors flyin' aroun'."

"But Paul's right. It's getting hard lots of places."

"Ah, you never know what gonna happen," Vasco said, dismissing the subject with a wave of the hand. "Just come in and work, maybe get a little overtime. Go home. What else you want?"

"Well, one thing for sure," Frank said. "I don't want to be laid off." He was a chunky man in his mid-thirties with thinning hair and gold-rim glasses.

"So what you want to *do?* Make the company close down, run away because you make lot of trouble," John said, speaking rapidly. "No thank you."

"You believe that?" Frank said.

"It *happens,*" John said. "I seen it happen myself."

"Company rumor," Stein said, his cigarette dangling from the corner of his mouth. "Just trying to make us get down on our hands and knees, saying how grateful we are just to have a job."

"But John's right about that one thing," Andy said. "They *do* close down shops. My brother was working in Revere. Whole plant shut down. Moved to Texas."

"Things *always* happen," Vasco said impatiently. "Rich man control things. Do what he wants. Layoff. Shutdown. Bang! You got to do your best, roll with the punch. Look out for number one."

"Can't we do more'n that?" Don asked. "Hell, we make the whole place run. . . ."

"You go ahead," John said. "You see what happens! You make trouble, see if you got a job. A lot of people got big ears here. And big mouths. . . ."

"Aw, John, relax," Frank said. "The kid's got a right to be worried. . . ."

There was an awkward pause.

"Well. . . ." Harry stood up and brushed the bread crumbs off his blue shirt and pants. "It's that time again." He sighed, then started moving toward the door.

The others got up too. Vasco chased after Harry and, dashing past him, flipped his hat up over his eyes. The others grinned. Vic moved away from the drafty window, folding his paper up carefully before he stuffed it into his pocket. He tossed his lunch bag in a cardboard box by the doorway and strode out, whistling to himself. Stein and Andy followed.

"Well. . . ."

"That time again. . . ."

Don started up, too. "Okay." He rolled his lunch bag into a ball and threw it in the box. Then he tucked his shirt in, wiped his mouth with his sleeve, and walked out. Frank followed.

Paul stayed on the floor, his head propped up on his long thin fingers. He took a cigarette from his pocket and lit it. A trail of lavender smoke curled around his face, up over his head. He inhaled deeply. The hum of the Banburies, silent during lunchbreak, started up again, whirring, wailing their high-pitched sound. The metal cans clattered along the rails. Harry's forklift truck barrelled down the hallway, making the floorboards tremble. It caught on a piece of metal and, dragging it, made a sudden sharp piercing noise, screeching, metal against metal, loud and scraping, a high grating sound which rose to a shrill peak, then abruptly stopped as quickly as it had begun. Paul winced.

Don lived with his wife Ellen in a small three-room apartment a mile from the plant, in the neighborhood they'd both grown up in. They'd been married a year. Ellen was training to be a nurse. They hoped that once both of them were working, they'd be able to put some money aside, pay Ellen's father back what he'd loaned them for her tuition, buy some new furniture, and maybe even move to a larger apartment. But for now, it was tough going.

When he came home from work that day, Don took a beer from the refrigerator, made himself a bologna sandwich and changed clothes. Flipping on the TV, he sat down across from it on a couch with a faded floral pattern and chewed on the sandwich, not really watching the program.

He'd run into an old friend on the way home from work. They'd talked about old times and what had happened to their pals. One had just broken his arm in a car accident. Another was in jail. Sammy, who'd played next to him on the high school football team, was working in a factory on the North Shore and going steady with a girl from Lynn. Riff was in New York; no one knew if he was ever coming back. Stan was working at City Hospital. Solly, the luckiest of the bunch, was going to the community college a few blocks away. As for the others, they were still on the street, drifting, getting high, stealing, living at home with parents who kept trying to kick them out. All that talk about what they were going to do . . . and none of them had done anything. It made him sad to think about it. His pals were good guys, with a lot of heart, a real love of life, lots of ambition. And now . . . .

Frank from work said this was the way the "system" operated; the rich didn't want working people to get ahead, and they ran things to make sure they wouldn't. Well, he couldn't argue too much with that.

His parents lived three blocks away in an apartment like his own. His father, disabled with a bad back, hadn't worked for seven years. His mother had a job for $2.60 an hour in a dressmaking shop nearby. His sister lived with them and gave them her paycheck every week. He tried to give $5 or $10 himself when he could. He knew he should be spending more time at their house, visiting and trying to cheer them up, but it depressed him to go there and hear his father's endless bitter tirades, see how weary his mother was, feel his sister's resentment.

He had his own family to think of now, too.

He glanced out the window. Snow had been falling steadily ever since mid-morning. The wind blew the flakes in swirls and made the windows rattle. The streets were full of people on their way home from work, some carrying shopping bags and packages, heads down, shoulders braced against the wind, pressing on towards their homes and families. It was getting dark.

He rubbed his forehead. Ellen should be coming home soon.

He was up for work the next morning at 5:30. The snow had stopped. It was clear and cold outside. He could hear the snowplows working to scrape away the snow, tossing steep ridges of grey crust and powder up along the roadsides, their chains clanking on the concrete streets.

He made himself a quick cup of coffee and a glass of juice, put on his work clothes and started out.

The sun was just coming up, a throbbing red ball just off the horizon. A few bands of pink clouds stretched above it, warming the eastern sky. In the west, the last few stars of night still glittered. The wind sliced through him as he walked, hunched over, hands stuffed into the pockets of his parka, feet crunching through the snow.

When he reached the plant, the coffee truck was outside the gate. John and Andy were there too.

"Hi. How ya doin'?"

"Enough snow for you?"

"Almost didn't get here."

"I know. There's going to be some people didn't make it

today."

"Hey! They better get the heat turned up in there!"

He stood in line, then got a cup of coffee and a cinnamon doughnut, and went in to work. Within five minutes he was at his machine. The Banbury motor was starting up again, feeder cans clattering, guillotine whirring away, Banbury gates slamming open and shut. Work as usual. . . .

A few minutes before 11:00, McNeil, the supervisor, walked over and tacked something up on the bulletin board. He looked at it, hands on his hips; then, apparently pleased with what he saw, he turned and walked away.

Vasco was the first to read it. "Hey, Don! You better read this. Hey, Paul! Where are you? Paul!"

McNeil sat at his desk in an office cubicle, shut off from the workers, reading the morning paper. A space heater throbbed and glowed bright orange. Outside, the work area was cold and drafty. Now that the snow had stopped, the temperature had fallen, and blasts of icy air rushed through the department through cracks in the windows and doors that had to be opened.

Don finished the batch he was working on, flipped the switch to "hold," and then went over to the board. McNeil had posted a notice:

To All Employees, Prep Department:

Because of declining production orders, it has become necessary to reduce the work force. This will be done in accordance with usual procedures as outlined in the Agreement between Management and the Local Union.

Effective Friday, February 17, 1978, the following workers will be terminated:

Carroll, D.	10357
Herrera, E.	10392
LaFleur, M.	10437
Santiago, J.	10266
White, R.	10398
Young, P.	10401

Signed: A. M. Roberts

He was being laid off! Along with five others in the department, he was being laid off. His name was at the top of the list. He read the notice all the way through again, a dull feeling expanding in his stomach. What was he going to do now? Where would he find another job, in the middle of winter? How was he going to pay his bills, meet the rent? Christ!

He walked slowly back to the Banbury, shaking his head.

"What is it?" Frank asked.

"They're laying off six guys. Two from each shift. I'm on the top of the list."

"You're kidding!"

"Some joke."

"Oh, Jesus." Frank paused and then asked, "Who else?"

"Paul. And the Spanish kid who runs the Ban second shift. And Roy."

"White?"

"Yeah. And two guys on third shift I don't know."

Frank clenched his teeth. "Just like those bastards. Send more work to Mississippi with one hand, and, with the other, lay us off."

The news spread quickly through the department. Everyone was talking about it.

"This is only the beginning."

"Aw, this place'll stay open till doomsday. They just want to shake us up."

"Go through this every year at this time."

"People'll get called back. Wait till the orders pick up. It's just slow now."

"You just got to wait and see. You never know. . . ."

"Hey," Harry asked, "has anyone told Paul?"

Don looked up. Paul was nowhere in sight.

"He's down by the locker room," Vasco shouted.

"I'll go tell him," Frank said, hurrying down the corridor. Soon Don saw the two of them walking back. "Paul!" he called.

"What?"

"I got it too." He went over to meet them.

Paul was standing in front of the notice. "Here's my name," he said, pointing to it. "But what do the rest say?"

"You can't read it?"

"Naw," he grinned, embarrassed. "I never learned."

Don read the notice out loud for him, then read it again. The corners of Paul's mouth fell. "When do it start?" he asked in a soft voice.

"Tomorrow."

"Tomorrow." He swallowed hard, then reached in his pocket for a cigarette. "Damn. What am I going to do? And me just four months off the unemployment line. . . ."

McNeil, watching from his warm cubicle, waved his arms.

"Let's all talk at lunch," Frank said.

McNeil opened his door. "Okay you guys. Back to work. Stop fucking around."

Don went back to work. From time to time he felt Frank looking at him, but he was angry and didn't want to talk to anyone. He stared straight ahead and worked mechanically, throwing the Banbury gate open with savage vengeance, slamming the cans down in their tracks, ripping the sacks of HiSil open with his knife as if they were McNeil himself.

At lunchtime they came together in the locker room.

"Well," Vasco said philosophically, "there it is. Layoff. What you going to say?"

"Nothing *to* say," Angel said. "They got no orders, so they got to cut down."

"What do you mean, no orders?" Frank asked. "They got orders enough to send work to Mississippi, measure the machines here so they can build more of 'em down there. They got plenty of orders. Only it's cheaper for them to send the work down there, where there's no union. . . ."

"They go through this every year," Vic said. "Ev-er-y year."

"Yeah. But this time it's coming down on *me!*" Don said.

"And on me," said Paul.

"You guys got lowest seniority. They just going by the rules," John said, spreading his lunch of chicken and rice neatly in front of himself. "It's in the contract."

"I read the contract," Don said. "It's their rules to start with."

"Well, we fought hard for that contract," Harry said, raising his eyebrows at Don as he opened up his carton of hot soup. "Johnny got us more money than we ever got before. . . ."

"Maybe it was a better deal," Andy put in. "But Don's right. The company uses that contract every day, to take money right out of our pockets, push us around."

"So what you going to *do* about it?" Vasco said. "They do what they want anyway."

"*What* you want union to do? They going by the book."

"Ain't there *somethin'* they can do?"

"Company got the right to hire and fire."

"Damn it," Don said. "Don't I have a right to keep my job?" They looked at one another.

"Not under this system, you don't," Frank said. "Like the man said, they can hire you and fire you whenever they want."

"What you want!" John exclaimed. "Whole plant shut down and everybody lose their jobs? Layoff is layoff. Collect for a few weeks, then they hire you back."

"The place *could* shut down, too. The way they're sending work to Mississippi."

"Johnny says we're lucky the whole plant *don't* shut down," Harry said. "Says him and the Executive Board are getting guarantees from the company right now."

"I don't think we need the union president to tell us that," Frank said. "We hear that from the company every day."

"Aw, it ain't so bay-udd," Pete said, trying to be reassuring. "Prub'ly call the both o' ya back in six weeks. Go home. You'll be ba-yuck."

"Yeah, sure," Don said. "Is there a guarantee on that one, too?"

Andy leaned forward. "I think everyone ought to have a right to a job. That's right. Ain't this the richest country in the world? So how come we got all this layoff, unemployment, plants shutting down?"

"Good question," Frank said. "In the meantime, you don't see profits falling. You notice that."

"Hey," Paul said suddenly, a worried look spreading across his face. "You mean there ain't nothing anyone can do?"

"Like they say," Stein said, coughing, his cigarette jammed in the corner of his mouth. "Things can pick up. Maybe they'll be calling you back in a month or so."

"They're laying off all over the place," Frank said. "Fifty here. Two hundred there. How're things going to get better?"

"Don't know, but they always do," Vic said.

"Do they?"

"Oh, sure. This is just temporary."

"I don't think so. Regal Shoes just ran away to New Hampshire. Fan-Tron shut down altogether. . . ."

"So what?" Vasco asked, exasperated. "What you going do about it besides talk?"

"What do *you* want to do about it?"

"Don't want nothing. I got my job."

"That's great," Don said. "Thanks. Today it's me. Tomorrow it could be you."

"Then I worry about it tomorrow!"

Paul shook his head. "We'd do better if we all stuck together."

Nobody said anything. The tension in the room rose.

"Yep," Andy said. "Rich get richer and the poor get poorer. We got to make the best of it. Stick together when we can. But damn, Don, I don't know what we *can* do this time around."

There was another pause.

"You know what I think?" Frank said. "I think a lot of people don't like these layoffs. But we don't have the *organization* we need to fight it. I mean, what's the union going to do when fifty more get laid off? Or when the whole damn shop is closed for good? When *are* they going to start fighting for us?"

"Right on!" Paul exclaimed. "Like, I'm down for fighting. But I know I can't do it by myself."

"I hear you," Andy said. "It's like Frank says. We got to have an organization to do somethin' like that."

"I thought that's what unions were for," Don said. "But I guess I'm learning something different."

"It *is* what unions are for," Frank said. "Only. . . ."

The others were quiet. Frank sighed and shook his head.

"Yup," Pete said. "We been through aw-ull this befower. When I was workin' in the mines 'fore I came here, we'd go on strike, get laid off. . . it don't never stop. 'At's what I think."

Vic sighed. "Well, it's that time again." He got up and folded his morning paper carefully, then put it in his pocket, then rolled his lunch bag into a ball and threw it into the cardboard box by the door. "Let's go."

Most of the men stood up.

"Hey, Don," Frank said. "Paul. Let's us get together after work, for a beer or something. Okay?"

"Okay. See you then."

About half an hour before lunch, Don heard shouts. He looked up and saw McNeil standing outside his office, hands on his hips, with Paul in front of him.

"I expect you to *move* when I say something!" he shouted.

"I'm doing my job!" Paul said. "You get the hell off my back!"

"I said clean that area. I expect it to be clean. You don't sit down until you've finished it."

"I was resting for a minute, man. Personal time. It's in the contract."

"Personal time, my ass! I call it loafing."

"Wait a minute. I got a right to a cigarette."

"And I don't want any back talk from you!"

"Oh, go fuck yourself!" Paul threw his broom halfway across the room. "You and this whole company! Treat people like they was dirt! Well, I'm a man, not some kind of animal!"

"You do your job, you won't get in any trouble. If you don't want to do your job, then punch out!"

"I didn't say. . . ."

"Look, Paul, I'm not going to discuss it. You get to work and sweep that floor. If you don't want to do it, punch out. I see that you're laid off as of tomorrow. Fine. If you want, you can quit today."

"Aw, McNeil, go back in your hole," Stein said loudly. "Can't we get some work done around here?"

McNeil glowered at him. "Herb, you stay out of this."

"Well, then, shut the fuck up! The guy's sweeping the floor. Let him sweep. Christ, get off his back!" Stein slammed a can against the railing. Then he slammed another.

Everyone was looking. Pete shut his Banbury off and walked over to where Paul's broom had landed. He picked it up and brought it to Paul, then stood next to him, round-shouldered, his stomach bulging out, his cap at an angle on his head. He was chewing on a wad of tobacco.

McNeil frowned. "All right, Paul," he said. "Now get yourself back to work."

Paul didn't say anything. McNeil was breathing heavily now.

"Let's go, Paul."

"Now, McNeil, you're gettin' yoursey-ulf aw-ull hot an' bothered," Pete said. "Ain' good fur your hey-ulth."

McNeil took out his handkerchief and swabbed his face. He looked around. All the workers were looking at him, bemused expressions on their faces.

There was a sudden rumble, as Harry's forklift truck came careening down the corridor, then screeched to a stop right in front of where McNeil and Paul were standing.

"Ain't nobody doing any work?" he said. "People stand around, somebody's going to get hurt." He swung himself down from the truck and looked at McNeil. "Got to keep these corridors clear," he said, shaking his head in a mock-serious way. "You know that."

McNeil bit his lip. "All right," he said. "Everybody get back to work." He turned and headed back to his office. "Let's go!" he bellowed.

Harry was laughing. "What the hell was all that about?"

"Bastard was riding me," Paul said.

"Take it easy," Pete said. "No sey-ense gettin' farred over that fool."

"It's just I didn't need him on me right then."

"That's what McNeil do all the time," Harry said. "He's one regular son-of-a-bitch. He'd just as soon get you to quit, so you couldn't get called back.

"Well. . . ." Paul turned and started back to where he'd left off sweeping the floor. He stopped a moment, reached in his pocket and took out a cigarette, then lit it. He leaned on his broom and turned around. "Say hey, Stein!" he shouted.

Stein grinned, then slammed another can against the rail and started singing loudly. Vic was whistling. Pete went over to the water fountain, then headed back to his Banbury.

"Aw-ull this startin' an' stoppin'," he said to Don. "Rooned another batch. Damn shay-yum. Ain' that right, Don?"

"Oh, yeah," Don replied. "But that's the way it goes."

"I guess it is," Pete said. "Damn shay-yum." He pulled the switch to start his machine up again.

When the shift was over, Don washed up and took his clothes and gear out of his locker. He took his $2.98 padlock off, too. The others came by to shake hands and wish him luck.

"Hey, Don, you been a regular guy."

"Take care of yourself."

"Hey, we'll probably be seeing you in a few weeks, anyway."

"See you later."

"Yeah. Okay. Thanks. See you around."

Then he was on his way down the dusty wooden steps again, perhaps for the last time.

Frank and Paul were at the gate. They walked up the street to a nearby bar, wrapping their coats tightly around them to keep the wind out.

"Hey, Paul," Don said. "That was some scene this afternoon."

"Damn bastard got on my nerves."

"Ol' Pete and Stein stood up for you, though. It was great! Sent McNeil right back into his hole."

"Uh-huh."

They entered the bar and found an empty table. Other workers from the plant were there, too, and they waved hello to them.

"Hey, you know what I heard?" Paul said after they'd sat down.

"What?"

"There's another fifteen laid off in the pressroom and the millroom. Some Black brothers and some of the Spanish people, mostly."

Frank clenched his teeth. "Damn!" he said. "And you know the union won't do a thing about it."

They ordered their beers, leaned back, lit up cigarettes.

"You can see what's going on," Frank said. "They'll keep laying off as long as they feel they can get away with it. Squeeze the last bit of work out of this plant and then move the whole operation down South."

"Why don't the union fight it?" Paul asked. "That's what I want to know."

"It's a long story," Frank said. "The bottom line is, folks like Johnny are bought and paid for by the company."

"For sure?"

Frank nodded. "They don't fight for us."

"But my dad helped organize a union where he worked before he got hurt," Don interjected. "People put their jobs on the line to get the union in. It must have been the same around here. So what happened?"

"Things got turned around. At first the factory owners tried to stop unions from coming in. When they saw they couldn't do that, they started buying off the leaders. I think that's what goes on, way at the top, with guys like Meany and Bommarito."

"But that puts the unions in the hands of the rich people instead of the workers," Paul said. "That ain't right. Folks like that, that won't stand up for the workers, we got to kick 'em *out* of the unions."

"That's how I see it, too," Frank said. "And that's why I think we got to build some kind of organization in the shop, *inside* the union." He paused to get a sip of beer. "Like, I talked to Andy after work. He doesn't like what's going on at all. I know he's ready to get together with other people who think the same way."

"There's a lot of people would join in," Paul said. Then he grinned, "Hell, if I ever do get back in myself, I'd be one right there."

"I know you would," Frank said.

"Things don't change overnight," Don said. "You heard a lot of those guys at lunch. They weren't ready to do anything except hold on to their jobs."

"They'll come around. If something gets going they will."

"If the whole plant closes, won't none of 'em have a job," Paul said.

Then they all ordered another round of beer.

"Well, what are you going to do, now you got time on your hands, Paul," Don said.

Paul made a face and shrugged. "I got to find a job," he said.

They stayed in the bar for another hour or so, talking about their plans, the factory, their families. Finally, Paul stood up and said he had to get home.

"Me, too," Don said. "I didn't know it was this late."

They paid their bill, then walked outside. The smell of the plant hit them right away, a sour smoky odor carried with the wind.

"See. You can't get away from it," Frank said, grinning. "It sticks with you like a glove."

"Uh-huh."

They shook hands with one another and separated.

"I'll give you a call," Frank shouted.

"Okay!"

"Take care."

Don started walking towards home, then realized he didn't want to go home yet. He wanted to walk. His mind was a jumble of thoughts and feelings, and he wanted time to sort them out. When he was younger, he used to take walks to think things through and that's what he wanted to do now. Turning away from the main square, he retraced his steps, passing the bar from the other direction. Soon he was in front of the plant.

The second shift was at work. Behind the plant, past the silhouettes of the smokestacks, the sky was clear. The sun was low in the west, casting fiery red reflections in the plant windows. Overhead, a low-flying jet roared past on its way to the airport, its harsh whine rattling the metal grillwork of the gate.

Don felt charged up. He stood with his parka half open, not minding the cold, staring at the factory, the snow lying frozen beneath his feet.

He was laid off. The fact hit him hard, like a blow to the chest.

He stood in the half-filled parking lot across from the shop, watching the smoke billow forth from the stacks, hearing the presses clang and the mills and Banburies chug. Men in the yard were shouting to one another.

A gust of wind blew directly at him, bearing the stench of the factory fumes. He grimaced and shook his head. Was he ever going to be back in there?

Walter Margolin, the skinny foreman in the pressroom and one of the most hated people in the plant, left the shop and climbed into his new Oldsmobile. The car started, then skidded on the snow as it sped out the gate and up the street. It raced up the hill, spewing chunks of frozen snow in its wake.

"Bastard," Don muttered to himself.

The bosses and supervisors parked their cars in a plowed lot inside the plant gate. The workers had to park in an unplowed lot across the street. One night, one guy working third shift had had all four wheels of his car stolen. But Walter Margolin's new Oldsmobile was always safe.

The guard at the gate had emerged from his small hut and was walking towards him. "Hey! Want something?"

"No."

"Your shift's over, ain't it? So beat it. Boss said he don't want anyone hanging around."

Don turned away, swearing to himself. So that was that. He started walking towards the river. So long, Banbury. So long, McNeil. So long, Vasco and Stein and Andy. . . .

The idea of getting together with Frank and some of the others suddenly appealed to him very much.

He moved ahead, stepping deliberately through the snow-splattered sidewalks, watching out for the pot-holes and slick spots, moving until he reached the river.

He stopped, looked at the small tenements perched atop the low hills across the way, near the airport. The river was dark and slick, oily. A tanker was heading out to sea; on deck, the sailors were moving about in green slickers. Far to the right, cars with their headlights on were crossing a bridge into the city.

Don started walking again, passing barges tied up by the docks, piles of wooden railings, fences, warehouses, gas stations, trucks. Another jet whined overhead, then thundered lower across the river towards its runway.

He passed beneath a highway which arched high above the slums, now filled with commuter traffic, workers like himself who had to drive miles each day to make a living, and who were now on their way home through the tangled lines of cars, horns blowing, windshields fogged up and icy, on their way to hot dinners at the family table. Other workers passed him, set looks on their faces.

He went past a Spanish grocery store, the police station, bars, vacant buildings, shops that nobody owned anymore, their windows boarded up. Then there was another factory where immigration authorities had come several weeks earlier seeking foreign-born workers. If he remembered right, the union there hadn't protected the workers at all, but had cooperated in fingering them to the cops.

He passed along an empty stretch of street, opening onto a vast wasteland that used to be the northern part of the town, before a fire had razed it several years ago. Buildings left standing had since been torn down, and the whole area was just brick and rubble, weeds and swampgrass.

Then he was at the old Farmers' Market, where produce for the city was hauled in; and then, curving along the road, he saw the Naval Hospital, on top of the hill to his left. Chemical factories stood in a line to his right. Ahead, the heavy concrete towers of the electric company rose up, purple lights flashing at their tops, signaling approaching planes, stark against the darkening western sky. Barbed wire ringed the plant's massive generators, tangle of wires, transformers, relays. The river twisted around one side of the plant, then continued on up into the valley beyond, past the tenements and factories, into the next town, and the town beyond that, the suburbs, and, finally, open country.

This was where he'd grown up. He and his folks had lived in this town all their lives, played in these streets, worked in these factories, lived in these buildings, shopped at these stores. This was what he knew. It was his life.

And now? . . .

Something was going on, something he didn't fully understand, but which was going on anyway. It was affecting every breath he took, every decision he made. And it wasn't just happening to him. It was happening to Paul, to four others in his department, twenty others in the plant . . . and how many others in the town he didn't even know about. It was affecting the workers who still had their jobs, just as much as the ones who'd been laid off. He'd never thought about these things before. But now. . . .

A truck bore down on him, its brights on. He jumped out of the way. Suddenly he realized he was cold. He'd been walking with his parka open. He pulled it around himself, buttoned it, pulled the collar up.

It was late.

Passing the candy factory where his sister worked, he moved up the hill towards his street, turned right and started down a thin slope.

Lights were on in most of the apartments up and down the block, making the windows into pale cats' eyes shining out on the snow-laden streets.

The wind was picking up again.

The Stranger

Pam held onto her relationship with Larry for three years, trying to help him kick the habit. Each time it seemed he'd done it, he'd be clean for two or three days, and then find a reason to disappear. When he'd come back, he'd be hooked again. Angry and disgusted, she'd retaliate by locking him out for a couple of weeks. But then he'd tearfully creep to her door, moaning and swearing to stay clean if she'd only help him "one more time." And she'd grit her teeth, shake her head and give in, devote the next few days to sticking it out with him, watching him cough and thrash about, tremble, shudder, twist, shriek.

It was always the same story. There never was a "last time."

Finally, even though she loved him and believed he was good, deep down, she broke it off. She told him she couldn't do it anymore, he was dragging her down. She said she'd never see him again.

"I can't be guilty about it. I got to save myself."

So she moved across town and got a job as a teacher's helper in a Head Start program. He disappeared. Soon after that, she found out she was pregnant. She worked until the eighth month, then took a leave of absence to have the baby, a girl she named Gretel.

When the girl was four months old, she got part-time childcare and went back to work.

Two years later, she met a quiet Black bus driver named Matt and fell in love with him. After a year they got married.

They saved their money and, when Gretel was eight, bought a house and moved to Allston. By this time she had two more children, both boys.

Matt received a promotion in the bus lines, but she sayed on at Head Start, where she'd gotten additional training so she could become a teacher herself.

People said they were a happy couple.

One day the phone rang, and when she picked it up there was no answer.

The next afternoon, when the children were playing in the backyard, Gretel came up to her, a worried look on her face.

"Mommy," she said, "there's a strange man."

"Where?"

"Leaning against a tree. Across the street. He keeps watching us."

She looked where the girl was pointing. A bearded man in jeans and a dark sweater was propped up against one of the trees across from her house, smoking a cigarette.

"Don't worry about it," she said. "He'll go away. Why don't you get Sammy and John and bring them inside to play awhile."

But the next day the man was there again.

"Why is he *watching* us?" the girl asked.

"I don't know."

When Matt came home from work, she told him about the stranger. But when he went to look, the man was gone.

The next day was Saturday, and Matt didn't have to work.

Just before ten o'clock, Gretel came running in again: "He's back, Mommy."

She sent Matt an anxious look, and he folded up his paper, laid it on his chair and headed for the back door.

Pam watched from the kitchen window. Matt crossed the backyard and cut through their neighbor's driveway, heading towards the street. The stranger was leaning against the same tree, dressed the same as before, smoking another cigarette.

Matt went up to the man and began talking. The man gestured. Matt kicked some dirt and put his hands in his pockets. The man shifted his weight, then leaned back against the tree. Matt shrugged, then shook his head. Then he started back towards the house.

The other man followed him, hesitated, then, when Matt motioned to him, began walking again.

The two of them crossed into the back yard together.

Then they were in the house.

Sammy and John were upstairs playing. Gretel suddenly dashed out of the kitchen and hid in the living room. Pam waited at the sink.

The door opened.

"May as well put some coffee on," Matt said coming in. He sat down and gestured to the stranger to sit down, too.

The stranger sat. He seemed uncomfortable, fidgeting in his chair and running his fingers jerkily over his russet beard.

"It's all right," Matt said quietly.

Pam put the coffee on, then lit a cigarette and sat down at the table.

The man had a long angular face, piercing brown eyes, a thin pinched nose and a small mouth.

"So it's you."

"Yes."

"I thought you'd gone for good."

"So did I."

She looked at him, saying nothing, remembering the months of torment they'd been through. His eyes were clearer now, but they had aged.

"You look well." She thought he looked thin.

He didn't say anything.

"I think he could stand a couple eggs. A sandwich maybe," Matt said.

She glanced at him, questioning him with her eyes.

"I could. That would be very kind. Thank you."

She got up quickly and took some eggs out of the refrigerator, mixed them in a bowl and put them on the stove to cook. She put some toast in, too. The men didn't speak. Gretel had sneaked to the other side of the kitchen door and was peeking through the edge. Pam put the plate of toast and eggs in front of him.

"Thanks." He picked up his fork and began to eat hungrily.

She poured a cup of coffee for each of them, let them help themselves to milk and sugar.

"What do you want?" she finally asked.

"I don't know. I guess I just wanted to see you. I heard there was a baby?"

"Yes."

"I don't want to make no trouble." He smiled awkwardly. "It's just. . . ." His voice trailed off, and the smile faded from his face. He was in the middle of a gesture and couldn't finish.

"It's been a long time," she said for him.

He gulped some coffee down. "I guess that's what it is," he said.

"You finally got off the drugs." She said it like a fact, not a question.

He nodded.

"That's good." She remembered the anger, pain and hate he'd aroused in her. "I'm glad for you."

"It's been two years," he said.

She nodded.

He wiped up his eggs with the toast, then washed them down with the rest of his coffee.

"That was good."

She poured him another cup.

Matt sat quietly, smoking his pipe, watching them. His coffee lay in front of him untouched.

"Can I see the child?"

She glanced at Matt.

"Okay."

She got up. Gretel, seeing her come towards the living room, shrieked and raced for the other side of the room.

"Gretel!"

"What?"

"Come here. I want you to say hello."

"No!" the girl dropped to the floor and buried her face in her hands. She was all curled up.

"Stop that! When I say something, you *do* it."

"I'm scared."

"There's nothing to be scared of. Come on."

She took her by the hand. The girl slowly stood up, smoothing down her dress. "All right." She started walking, then stopped, pulling away and turning her head. "Do I have to?"

"Uh-huh."

She led her firmly. The girl came with her across the living room, through the doorway, into the kitchen.

The man looked at her, gazing at her long blond-red hair, color of his own; her small frightened mouth; pale arms, wrinkled dress, bony knees, white socks and black patent leather shoes.

"Come closer, honey."

She looked at her mother.

"It's okay."

She stepped towards him.

The man reached out and touched her on the arm. She trembled a little, but left it there. He slid his fingers down her arm and clasped her fourth and fifth fingers with his hand. Then he let go.

He stood up suddenly:

"I got to go."

He was moving towards the door.

"Larry!"

Wide-eyed, he stared at the three of them: the Black man

holding his pipe, the woman and the girl. Then he turned and fled through the open door.

Pam heard him cry out as he ran across the yard. The sound pierced her like a needle, touching memories buried for years.

She knew he'd never stop running.

Gretel was hugging her frightened.

"Don't worry," she said, her eyes moist. "He wouldn't have hurt you."

She turned to Matt. "You did okay, honey. Thanks."

"Poor son of a bitch," Matt said.

The girl looked for him for the next couple of days and for a week after that; but, as he didn't come back, she stopped looking.

She never forgot the touch of his hand on her arm.

Down
at the Line

At nine o'clock on a cold morning, a man walked down Grant Street towards the unemployment office, shoulders hunched up and neck tucked down against his leather jacket. Above him, the sun was a pale silvery disc in the east, hovering over the tenement roofs, barely visible behind a band of grey clouds. A sharp wind, dry and cutting, blew in from the northeast. Overhead, three subway cars clattered on their way to Pond Station. Glancing up, the man reflected he'd have been on them, but he didn't have a quarter.

He turned to look back. His wife would be bustling around the apartment now, straightening up. The boy would be in the kitchen, the only warm room in the house, finishing his oatmeal and playing with his toy cars. The refrigerator was empty. They had no money for food or rent, or to get the heat back on.

He reached automatically in his pocket for a cigarette. Then, remembering he didn't have any, he made a face, gritting his teeth together and tightening his lips. He shook his head and started walking again.

He was a slim man in his early twenties, dressed in blue jeans, a grey sweater on top of a flannel shirt, a leather jacket, and a blue sailor's cap. His face was narrow and rough, high cheekbones accentuating his deepset brown eyes. His complexion was pitted. He had a flat, crooked nose (twice broken, once playing ball and once earlier in a fight) and thin, tapered lips which gave his mouth an intense, though not humorless, expression.

He walked deliberately. It had been nine weeks, and he'd yet to get one check.

A gust of wind made him suddenly bend forward, hands jammed in his pockets, head down. Jesus, it was cold! His eyes began to tear, and his nose started running. He still had a couple blocks to go.

He was hungry. But, more than that, he was angry. For nine weeks he'd shown up faithfully to sign the sheet, asking for money that was rightfully his. And for nine weeks he'd gotten nothing, not even a courteous answer. Just red tape. The runaround. He'd been laid off his job in the factory, but the boss told unemployment he had been fired for poor attendance. So the claims person said he couldn't collect until this was cleared up, and wrote his boss to send in some forms, but in the meantime he had to come in every week and sign up or lose the claim.

He'd borrowed all the money he could from his brother and a few friends, and now he was flat broke. He'd looked for a job and couldn't find one.

He walked past a row of small stores, half of them boarded up, graffiti in chalk and black paint all over the walls, and the ruins of an apartment building, now just a heap of rubble on the ground. The whole area was falling apart. Nobody would spend the money to save it. Stores were left vacant. Buildings were burned down by their owners. Streets were never cleaned.

Another train passed overhead, traveling in the opposite direction. Its grumbling noise crested to a roar as it neared him, blasting his ears, then fell suddenly, passing, moving away, dropping gradually to a dull, distant growl, an echo of itself.

Things were falling apart. He needed his check desperately.

Finally he reached the unemployment office, a low one-story brick building which had been used as a factory outlet until the state took it over. The parking lot was already half full.

As he turned in, a young Black man with a handful of leaflets approached him. "Hey, brother," he called. "Leaflet on the crisis? See how we can fight. . . ."

"Later," he said, pushing ahead. "In a hurry."

"Okay." A nod of the head. "Catch you later."

He took a deep breath, then let it out, the steam making a thin white cloud over his head. He didn't need any damned leaflet. He needed his check or a job.

He went through the glass doors into the building. Lines of twenty and more people stretched out before each claims window. He took his place at the end of the third one, fingering the ID card in his pocket and the folded-up weekly report sheet he'd filled out at home before leaving. His fingers were numb from the cold,

Some of the people in line were familiar to him by now.

"Hi."

"How you doing?"

"Back again?"

"Uh-huh."

"Bitch outside, ain't it?"

"Cold as hell."

"Hey. But you got to eat."

"If you can get your check."

"That's right." A pause. "Hey, you ain't got your check yet?"

"Naw. I been here nine weeks. . . ."

"I thought I'd seen you a couple times."

". . . and not a check yet."

"Damn! Well. . . ." The line moved. "Good luck with it today."

"Thanks. I'll need it."

He hated the line. It embarrassed him being there, like it was somehow his fault he didn't have a job, an admission of personal failure. He knew it wasn't so, but that was how he felt, because that was how they treated him. Some of the other men, especially the ones there for the first few times, felt the same way. He could tell by the way they stuck by themselves, quiet, eyes staring ahead or at the floor, or glancing at the walls, at the out of date yellow notices, anything to avoid other people's eyes. It was humiliating, no matter how you cut it.

The clerks didn't make it any easier. All they knew you by was your name and number, and they couldn't care less about the rest. Just a few weeks ago, he'd seen the manager call the cops on a Puerto Rican man who'd gotten angry and was shouting at the woman behind the claims window. The cops had handcuffed him and dragged him away while everyone else looked on.

The line inched ahead. As they waited, some of the "regulars" took up conversations they'd left off the previous week.

"So how's your mother?"

"Aw, about the same, I guess."

"Still coughing a lot?"

"Oh, yeah."

"Did she ever get that doctor?"

"Finally. She didn't want to go, you know. But then me and my sister dragged her out, put her in a cab and drove her to the doc. Damned doc made her wait over an hour. Then he says she got to take this medicine regularly. Gave her antibiotics, and something else for when she gets short of breath."

"Uh-hu. Well at least she seen him."

"Uh-huh." A pause. "Hey, you see that show on TV last night? About the kids with drug problems?"

"No, I missed that one."

"Well, they showed this one kid, couldn't have been more than thirteen. . . ."

The line moved ahead again. Now he could see his claims clerk, a woman about thirty in a white blouse and skirt with glasses. Just one or two more people to go, and then it was his turn. His heart was beating fast. He just *had* to get his check this week.

The woman had a box of folders in front of her, and a stack to her right where she put the folders of people she'd seen. She had a cup of coffee and a half a doughnut. It reminded him how hungry he was.

Then it was his turn: "Lloyd. Walter." He pushed his ID card and weekly report slip through the window.

The woman took his folder out of the box.

"So. . . . have they got this thing settled yet?" he asked.

"What thing?"

"About my being laid off. So I can collect." He tried to smile, but couldn't.

"Just a minute. . . ." She leafed through the folder. "The required statement from your employer is still not here. I have a note saying that we wrote him for it, but he hasn't answered it yet."

"That's what you said a week ago."

"Well, I'm sorry. We'll still have to wait for it." She pushed the signature sheet through the window to him. "Sign here, please, and you'll have to come back next week. Maybe then there'll be something further. . . ."

"I been coming for nine weeks," he said, his voice strained, his head pounding. "I haven't seen a check yet."

"I understand that Mr. Lloyd. But there's nothing I can do. Your employer has to. . . ."

"Well, what is he *waiting* for! You wrote him *weeks* ago!"

"You'll have to ask *him* that."

"And what am I supposed to use to pay my rent, or buy food? . . ."

"I don't know." A pause. "Have you been down by the welfare office?"

"No."

"Then I suggest you go down there. They have an emergency program. Now, if you'll move along. . . ." She slapped his file down on the stack of people-seen folders.

"I don't *want* to go to welfare," he said. "I want my check. I got a right to it."

She was getting flustered. "I can't do anything about that. If you have a complaint, you'll have to try window seven."

"I was there last week, and they didn't do anything."

"Well. . . ."

"Well, look. . . ." he stammered. His mind was suddenly a

jumble. What did they *want* from him? He deserved his check. Why couldn't he get it? Other people in line were staring at him, and his face was getting red.

"I just don't see why I can't get my check," he said. "Okay?" He leaned forward, his hands tight on the ledge in front of the window. "All I'm asking for is money I got a right to. . . ."

"Please move on," she said. "There are other people behind you."

He hated her. But she wasn't the main one. How do you cut through all the red tape and grab the people who are out to destroy your whole life?

Suddenly, out of the corner of his eye, he saw another clerk motion to the cop. He had to think fast now. Either he moved on, or he'd be in jail.

Christ! He couldn't get arrested with no food in the house, not when he could still try welfare, maybe get day work. If he was single, yes, go ahead, let it all hang out; but now he had the responsibility for his family and he couldn't go off half-cocked like he used to.

"Mr. Lloyd?"

"What?"

"So you'll come back next week, and we'll try and have you answer for you?"

It was more than he could handle. They had him. "Okay," he mumbled, defeated. He took his hands off the ledge and turned around, walked back between the lines of people who were watching him. His ears burned. Jesus! They knew more ways to humiliate a man. He was like a hamster in a cage, running around a wheel. Run and run and never get anywhere, and in the meantime someone else gets rich off it. It made him sick.

He shoved the glass doors open so hard they slammed back against the sides of the building. Back in the cold again, the wind lashing his jeans against his legs, his red face stinging. Damn! He kicked a stone and watched the pigeons scatter, then began walking through the parking lot. He'd have to tell Annie about this and try and figure out what to do. Maybe she could go to welfare while he looked for day work . . . but they had to find a couple bucks for food, somehow.

He walked back towards Grant Street, kicking the stone hard when he came to it again. It flew all the way to the street.

". . .mad as hell." Someone was talking to him. The young Black man with the leaflets.

"What?"

"I said, something heavy must have gone down in there, 'cause you look mad as hell."

"How would *you* feel if you'd been coming nine straight weeks and never got one check!" he said angrily. "Shit!"

"I guess I'd be pissed off like you," the man said. "Hey, what's the story? How come they messing with you like that?"

He was a tall skinny Black youth dressed in denim, with a sailor cap like Wally's. Why would a Black guy give a damn about him? In this city?

"No story to tell," Wally said, feeling him out. "I got laid off, but the boss lied, said I was fired."

"You got witnesses?"

He hadn't thought about that. "Sure."

"And the boss hasn't sent in the form. Right?"

"Right. Every week I come and sign, and every week I get nothing. Hey, I got a wife and kid, and we ain't got a dime."

"I hear you. Hey," he suddenly held out his hand, "my name is Paul."

He decided Paul was okay. "Wally." They shook hands.

"You know," Paul said, "this don't happen just to you. Lots of people don't get their checks when they should. The system's got all kinds of red tape to mess you up. But that boss of yours had two weeks to get his shit together. After that, the law says the unemployment's got to make a determination."

"They ain't made no determination," Wally said bitterly. "Just told me to keep coming in, week after week."

Paul thought a minute. "Well, that ain't right," he said. "They ain't even going by their own rules on this one." He grinned. "Well, what do you say? Are you down for fighting it, or you just want to go home?"

"What do you mean, 'fighting it'?" Wally asked.

"I mean, going in there and fighting for your check. You got a right to it, don't you?"

"For sure."

"Well?"

'Well, we just don't go in and *ask* for it," he said sarcastically. "I just done that."

"We can go in with you," Paul said. "We done it before. That's why they're always hassling us out here. Trying to keep us out of the parking lot, off the street, away from the door. . . .They know we fight their bullshit."

Another subway train passed overhead, making so much noise they had to stop talking for a minute.

"Wait a second," Wally said when it had passed. "Who's this 'we'?"

"Right. I'm a member of the Fight Back Organization," Paul said. "We got chapters all over the United States. Like, fighting for jobs. Fighting against discrimination. Fighting layoffs."

"Uh-huh."

"We're down here a couple times a week." He paused. "You ever get one of our leaflets?"

"Naw. I don't think so. I mean, maybe I took one, but. . . ."

"But you didn't read it. Right?" He grinned.

"Right."

"Well, hey, take one now and look it over when you got the time. It tells what we're all about. How we got this campaign for jobs in the city. Jobs at *union* wages, that is." He shook his head. "I keep forgetting that part of it. I just been doing this a couple weeks myself, and I don't have the whole rap down yet, if you know what I mean."

"You're doing okay, seems to me," Wally said. Paul reminded him of a friend from work.

"Well, let's talk it over with the other folks." He turned. "Hey! Ron! Sally!"

"What?" They were two people talking to someone in the parking lot.

"Come here a minute. Got to talk."

"Okay." They came up. "What's up?"

"This is Wally," Paul said.

"Ron."

"Sally."

"Right." They all shook hands.

"Hey, let's go across the street and get a cup of coffee if we're going to talk," Ron said. "Damn, it's too cold to stand out here."

"Now you're talking," said Paul, banging his hands together.

There was a small coffee shop across the street. Wally hesitated. "I ain't got a cent," he said. "That's why I'm. . . ."

"Forget it," Ron said. "We can swing it."

They went in and ordered cups of steaming hot coffee and a couple doughnuts fresh out of the oven, and then they sat down and Paul and Wally explained the situation. The others listened patiently as they went over all the different details.

"And Wally says he's down for going in," Paul concluded. "That's right?"

"If you think it'll do any good, sure," Wally said. "All I know is I can't do it myself. And I sure do need that check."

"Okay." Ron lit up a cigarette. He was a serious-looking guy with dark curly hair and thick black eyebrows. "So how do we do it?"

"Let's go to window seven," Sally said. "And demand to see Mr. Marinaro. It doesn't make sense to go to Wally's claim window. It'd just tie people up. And we couldn't get an answer from the clerk." She was an older woman with a round face, short brown hair. Seemed like a lawyer or something, the way she talked.

"Okay. So who's going with Wally?"

"Why don't I go," Paul said. "Ron can talk to the people. Sally, you can come with us, just in case we get too steamed up." He chuckled, looking forward to the scrap.

"Sounds good. Let's do it."

"Let's go."

They headed back across the street.

Wally was excited. Goddamn! This was something else. He couldn't wait to see the expression on that woman's face when he came back in. And here were three people he'd only just met, who were willing to take up a fight for him. How about that? Even if he didn't win his check, it was worth it.

It was close to ten-thirty now, and the parking lot was full. They crossed it quickly, entered the building, and went straight to window seven.

The clerk seemed to know them. "Yes?"

"We're here about Mr. Lloyd's claim," Sally said.

"And which one is Mr. Lloyd?"

"That's me," Wally said.

"All right. Why don't you give me the necessary information. Your friends can wait over there."

"We're waiting right here," Paul said loudly. "We're waiting right here until Mr. Lloyd gets his check, which he deserves."

"If you people aren't putting in a claim yourselves, you can't be here," the clerk responded.

"That's not true, and you know it," Sally said. "We have a right to be here as Mr. Lloyd's agents. Could we please speak with Mr. Marinaro?"

The clerk was already rattled. "I think he's busy. I'll get the information myself."

"But you're going to have to call Mr. Marinaro sooner or later. Right? So why not now?"

People were beginning to stare.

"Uh, Sharon," the clerk called to a woman behind him. "Would you tell Mr. Marinaro we may need him."

"Okay."

"Now," he said, in a peevish voice. "Your name is. . . ."

"Walter Lloyd. My file's at window three. I was just over there."

"Okay." He looked for a pencil, then put it down. "Just let me take a minute. . . ." He left to get Wally's file.

"What now?" Wally asked.

"Nothing. Just hold tight."

The clerk returned. "All right," he said, smoothing his mustache. "Now let's see. You're waiting for a determination."

"Uh-huh."

"Well," he tried to smile at them, "I just don't see what we. . . ."

"The point is," Wally said, "I've been waiting for nine weeks. That's not right!"

"But your boss hasn't mailed in the right form," the clerk said in a helpless tone.

"That's tough shit," Paul said. "No reason for Wally to be messed up 'cause of that. You got to make your determination anyway."

"He said he was laid off."

"I *was* laid off."

"The boss doesn't agree."

"So two weeks is up," Paul said. "What do *you* say?"

More and more people were watching. Suddenly, Ron, who was standing in an area in the back of the office, held his arms up and started speaking in a loud voice to the people around him. "Folks. This man is being given the *shaft*. He was laid off. And he's been waiting *nine* weeks for his check. *Nine weeks!* He doesn't have *food* in his house, no *money* in his *pocket*. And they're giving him the *runaround*. We're from the *Fight* Back, and we say give the man his *check.*" He spoke in a quick staccato voice, leaning heavily on certain words.

People turned around to listen.

"Aw, shut up," someone said.

But Ron went on. "This has been happening a lot. You know that. Maybe some of *you* had to wait six, eight, maybe ten weeks for your first check. You can understand what this fellow, *Wally,* is going through." He raised his arms higher, whirling about to address the different people who were now looking at him.

"You've seen us in here before. And you know we're not just trouble-makers. We're here fighting for people's rights! That's why we say, give this man his check! Will you support us?"

"All right! Give the guy his check," someone said. "What the hell."

"I'll go along with that," someone else added.

Wally saw a man in a suit go over to the cop, and then the cop nodded and disappeared. To make a phone call, he wondered.

Sally saw the man, too. "Oh, Mr. Marinaro," she called, "now that you've called the police, maybe you could come over here. That's the office manager," she explained to Wally.

The man turned, then moved towards them. He was a chubby man with a pencil thin mustache, all dressed up in a natty brown checkered suit. "All right, Stan," he said. "I'll handle this." He cleared his throat, then looked at Wally with a quick phony smile and picked up his file.

"Mr. Lloyd?"

"That's me," Wally said. He was struck by how small and clean the man's hands were.

"Yes?"

"I been waiting nine weeks for my check, and now I get told I could have had it two months ago."

"The employer hasn't written back," the clerk whispered. "Form 119. So there hasn't been a determination."

"We're waiting for a report from your employer," Mr. Marinaro said, as if he was explaining something to Wally he didn't know.

"I *know* that," Wally exclaimed. "But you had two weeks!"

"In some cases, it's true, it does stretch out. But, while it may be inconvenient. . . ."

"Inconvenient!" Wally cried. "I ain't got money to eat!"

"We want to be as fair as possible, to both sides concerned."

"What kind of bullshit is that?" Paul cried. "You folks aren't in the middle. Since when were you in the middle?"

"Just give me my check," Wally said. "You've had nine weeks to decide. Now you have to say yes or no. It's that simple. I worked for my check. I'm entitled to it. But it seems you won't give a man what's his."

"That's right," Ron called.

"Hey, give the man his check," an older Black woman called out. "These people are right."

Just then there was a shriek of police sirens, and two cars pulled up at the door. They emptied quickly. Six cops rushed in, night sticks in their hands.

The cops looked to Mr. Marinaro for orders. "You got a problem here?" the sergeant asked.

"We'll know in a minute. Look," he said to Wally, lowering his voice. "I don't want to have a scene here. Perhaps you'd like to come into my office?" He was sweating.

"Then we come, too," Sally said quickly.

Mr. Marinaro hesitated. The room was dead quiet. A

hundred and fifty people were watching what was going on. All the lines had stopped moving.

"Give the man his check and get on with it," someone suddenly called from the other end of the room.

"Give him his check."

"Give him his check." Voices rose up from all sides.

"If you people stand with him, he *will* get his check," Ron said. "You *know* he can't do it on his own."

Several people on the lines nodded their heads.

The cops moved closer. Three of them surrounded Ron, sticks in hand. "You shut up," one of them said, "or you'll be in for inciting to riot."

"Hey. Free speech." Ron said. "The people here say give the man his check, and I say it too." His voice rose. "Give the man his check!"

"Give the man his check!" a woman cried out.

"Give the man his check!"

The cops moved on Ron. "Let's go." They grabbed him. Ron tried to shake free. One cop raised his club.

"Leave him alone!" Wally shouted. "He hasn't done anything wrong!"

Ron twisted away, receiving the blow on his shoulder. Another smacked him in the back.

"Leave him alone!" several people shouted at once.

"Leave him alone!"

"Get him out of here, boys," Mr. Marinaro said.

The cops began to drag Ron away, but people from the lines surged forward.

"Hey, let him loose!"

"He ain't done nothing!"

"Leave him alone!"

A lot of angry people were ready to stop the cops. Wally felt his throat go dry. His head pounded.

"Wait a minute," Mr. Marinaro said, quickly and loudly. "Um, wait a minute."

The cops stopped. Ron twisted in their grip. Mr. Marinaro cleared his throat. "Er, I think we can handle this ourselves, officers. Why don't you hold up a minute."

They let Ron loose.

Mr. Marinaro raised his small clean hands. "Come on folks," he pleaded. "Let's break it up. Can we get back to handing out the checks? We'll handle this man's claim."

"Just give him his check," a voice said.

"That's right. Give him his check."

"Give him his check."

"Okay. I'll take one of you in the office with him, but not both," Mr. Marinaro whispered hastily. "Okay?"

"Okay. Why don't you go?" Paul said to Sally.

She accompanied Wally into the office. The policemen stayed in the back of the room, glaring at Ron and Paul.

"Next time," one of them muttered, "I'm going to bust that commie's head."

Mr. Marinaro's office was pastel blue. He had a large wooden desk and several comfortable curved-back chairs with blue cushiony seats. He motioned to them to sit down.

"I don't know what it is with you people," he grunted. "Always making trouble. Almost had a riot on our hands out there. Next time, believe me, someone's going to get arrested for it. But. . . ." He held his finger in the air to indicate he was going to keep talking. "It looks like you might have, er, hit on a shortcoming in Mr. Lloyd's case." He placed the folder on his desk and opened it up again.

"Seems pretty simple to me," Wally said.

"Er, um, you were laid off, you say?"

"Yes sir. Ask anyone there."

"Mmm-hmm." He scribbled something in the file. "And I see you've been here every week, signing up."

"That's right."

"Well. . . ." He sighed. "Excuse me for a minute." He got up and cleared his throat again, and then went next door to another office. They could see him making a phone call.

"It's going all the way to the district manager," Sally said. "He's done this before."

"It's like some kind of game. . . ."

"I know. He really hates our guts. Two weeks ago we had to bring a lawyer down here."

"Wow." He couldn't forget what had happened outside. "Weren't the people out there really great? Everyone calling out. He didn't know what to do."

"Uh-huh."

"I never thought people would do that."

"They're in the same situation you are. And, see, we've been doing work here for almost a year. Things have been building up."

Mr. Marinaro finished his conversation and hung up the phone. He went into yet another office, carrying Wally's file with him, then finally started back towards them.

He was half out of breath. "All right, Mr. Lloyd," he said, "You'll have your checks in a few minutes. I am sorry you had to wait all this time." It was clear that was all he had to say. He stood up and extended his hand to Wally. "If you'll just wait here, the girl will be in with your checks."

Wally shook the hand, then wondered why he had. But by then, Mr. Marinaro was out the door.

"Is that it?"

"I think so. Looks like we won." Sally smiled and lit up a cigarette.

"Hey, that's really great." He felt light-headed. "Say, can I bum a cigarette from you? I think I'll be able to pay you back."

"Sure."

While they were smoking their cigarettes, a young Black woman came in: "Mr. Lloyd?"

"Like I say, that's me."

"Here's your checks. You get nine weekly payments at eighty-six dollars a week. That comes to $765." She handed him nine checks.

He looked at them. Beautiful government grey, with his name and social security number on it.

"Oh, Jesus," Wally said, "we really did it!"

"Let's go tell the others."

They walked out into the main room. The police were gone. Ron was handing out leaflets to the people in the different lines, while Paul was in the back, talking to two young Black men.

"Hey! We won!" Wally cried, waving the check in the air.

154

"Here it is!" He grinned, and people grinned back.

"All right!"

"Atta boy!"

"Don't spend it all tonight, now."

Ron slapped him on the back. "All right! How about that!"

"Hey. How are you? Are you hurt?"

"No. I'm okay. But, I tell you, if the people hadn't taken it up when they did, I'd be down at the station now, all black and blue."

"I know. It was beautiful what happened."

"Wasn't it? Hey, we've been here almost a year, and this is the best that's ever happened. I can't believe it myself!"

"Hey!" He snapped his fingers. "I got to tell Annie."

"Okay. I'm about ready to go, too. Paul, you ready?"

"You go ahead," Paul said. "These brothers and I are into some heavy talking. Catch you later."

"Paul. Thanks," Wally said. "I really appreciate it."

"You'll be helping us out sometimes. Right?"

"For sure. I'll catch you at one of these meetings."

"Out of sight!"

They walked out. Once again, it was the wind and cold, but this time he didn't mind.

"Okay. You better get those checks home now," Sally said.

"I will. Jesus!"

"Let me give you my phone number," Ron said searching his pockets for a pencil and a piece of paper. "And I want to get yours, too. Maybe we can get together later this week. There's a lot I'd like to tell you, about what we're doing."

"I'd like that." They exchanged numbers. "When did you say your meetings are?"

"Sundays. At three."

"Maybe Annie and I can both come. I'll talk to her about it."

"Fine. Sally, you staying?"

"Uh-huh. I think I'll hand out a few more leaflets and talk to the people coming out."

"Okay. I'll stick with you."

"Okay. So long," Wally said. "And thanks again."

"So long, Wally. See you soon."

He turned and started back up Grant Street, following the line of the elevated subway train. He was on his way back home again, the checks in his back pocket. He walked fast, hands in his pockets, his mind going over all the things that had happened, the new friends he had made, the struggle with the cops, the way all the people had supported him. It was really something! He'd see that expression on Mr. Marinaro's face for the rest of his life, the sheepish look when he told him he'd be getting his checks. Goddamn! That was one good victory to put next to a whole bunch of defeats he'd been handed lately. And he was interested in hearing more about this Fight Back group. But that could wait till tomorrow. Right now, he was going home to tell Annie and Jon about the checks, and then they were going to buy some food and beer to celebrate. What the hell! He'd earned himself the right to a good dinner. And he'd just remembered again how hungry he was.

$3.95

In Boston, the segregationist movement is at its height, and a Black family becomes the target of gang violence in a white neighborhood. "Trouble on the Hill," the title story, shows the complex situation that develops when one neighbor gradually comes to take their side.

As a single mother moves her family to make a new start, her 11-year-old son enters a lonely childhood of welfare, racism and schoolyard fights, finding strength and the early maturity of city youth.

An Indian mother fights to keep custody of her infant son; a rubber worker faces layoffs as his factory threatens to close down; an unemployed worker fights to get his check at an unemployment office. . . .

These are the people of Michael Glenn's first book of fiction, working and poor people described with a realism suited to the America of the seventies. These stories show us the anger, awareness and character taking shape today in our cities and factories.

"They are great proletarian stories, like the young Jack London or Gorki. They are so absolutely right in class feeling and told like mystery stories, really grabbing your attention."

Meridel Le Sueur,
author of Salute to Spring

"Michael Glenn is the sort of writer I used to look for when I was publishing *The Anvil*. His style is straight and dramatic and holds the interest of the serious reader who is still concerned with the workers' world."

Jack Conroy,
author of The Disinherited

MICHAEL GLENN is a founder of *The Radical Therapist* magazine, co-author of *Repression or Revolution: Psychotherapy in the U.S. Today,* and editor of the collections, *Voices from the Asylum* and *The Radical Therapist*. His stories have appeared in *The Hudson Review, The Antioch Review,* and the anthology, *Young American Writers*.

A community activist, Glenn has also worked in a number of factories and hospitals in the Boston area.

Cover design by Julie O'Connor   0-930720-61-X

Liberator Press, P.O. Box 7128, Chicago, Il. 60680